"What sort of clothes do you want me to buy? Something to titillate you?"

"You don't need clothes to do that."

Her face burned. "I can't do this," Anna said with a helpless flutter of her hands. "I can't pretend to be your mistress like this."

"You will not be pretending," Lucio assured her. "I will make sure of that."

She stared at him in consternation. Was that to be his final revenge? To have her want him and love him all over again…?

MELANIE MILBURNE says, "I am married to a surgeon, Steve, and have two gorgeous sons, Paul and Phil. I live in Hobart, Tasmania, where I enjoy an active life as a long-distance runner and nationally ranked top-ten Master's swimmer. I also have a master's degree in education, but my children totally turned me off the idea of teaching! When not running or swimming, I write, and when I'm not doing all of the above I'm reading. And if someone could invent a way for me to read during a four-kilometer swim I'd be even happier!"

Melanie Milburne

THE ITALIAN'S MISTRESS

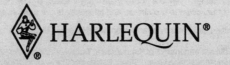

TORONTO • NEW YORK • LONDON
AMSTERDAM • PARIS • SYDNEY • HAMBURG
STOCKHOLM • ATHENS • TOKYO • MILAN • MADRID
PRAGUE • WARSAW • BUDAPEST • AUCKLAND

To my son Paul,
you have taught me so much about courage, conviction and computers. I dedicate this book to you for the hurdles you have overcome while we watched on the sidelines in awe.

ISBN 0-373-18859-5

THE ITALIAN'S MISTRESS

First North American Publication 2005.

Copyright © 2004 by Melanie Milburne.

CHAPTER ONE

ANNA stared at her son's specialist in horror. 'You mean he's…going to *die*?'

The doctor's expression was grave. 'Without the necessary private insurance your son will have to wait a year, if not eighteen months, for his surgery in the public system.'

'But I can't afford private insurance.' Anna's stomach tightened with worry. 'I can barely afford to feed us both as it is!'

'I realise the difficulties single mothers such as you face,' he said with little trace of the empathy she craved. 'But the public system is already overloaded and close to collapsing. Your son's condition is not life-threatening in the short term—however, the hole in the heart needs to be repaired before permanent damage is done.' He gave the notes on his desk a small shuffle before adding, 'If you can raise the necessary funds through some sort of benefactor the surgery could be done within the month at the Melbourne Centre for Heart Surgery.'

Anna's heart sank. She could barely afford the tram fare to the city let alone an operation carried out in one of the nation's premier hospitals.

'How…much would it cost?' she asked, unconsciously edging closer to the edge of her seat.

He appeared to be doing some sort of mental calculation before he named a figure that nearly sent her off the chair to the carpeted floor beneath her.

'*That much?*' she gasped.

'I'm afraid so. Sammy would be in hospital at least ten days, which drives up the costs considerably. And if there are complications…'

5

'Complications?' She swallowed the lump of dread in her throat. 'What sort of complications?'

'Miss Stockton, any surgery carries risks. Delicate heart surgery on a three-year-old child is fraught with difficulties—infection, for one thing, not to mention adverse reactions to drugs and so on.' He closed the file on his desk and, leaning back in his chair gave her his version of an encouraging smile. 'I suggest you go home and ring around all your friends and relatives and hunt for someone who will foot the bill. It's your son's best chance of a quick and successful outcome.'

Anna gave an inward sigh as she got to her feet. As far as relatives went she had very few apart from her sister...And her friends?

When she'd come rushing back from overseas four years ago the last thing she had been thinking about was building a network of supportive friends; all she could think about was putting as much distance as possible between herself and the Ventressi family.

Hardly a day went past when she didn't think of her ex-fiancé Lucio, and his brother, Carlo...

No!

She wrenched her mind away from those terrible memories...the realisation of what she'd done...those horrible accusations that still rang inside her head if she allowed herself to think back...

The busy city street was packed with scurrying crowds of people trying to weave their way in and out of shops and businesses, the unseasonable November heat only adding to their general impatience.

Anna thought longingly of a cold drink. Checking her watch, she saw she had at least an hour before she had to make her way to the tram to take her back to her little son, Sammy, and Jenny, her younger sister.

She saw a coffee shop in the distance and made her way to it determinedly. Her throat was dry, her cheap cotton blouse wet between her shoulder blades and, as she went past a window, she saw that her blonde hair was lying about her shoulders in limp strands, giving her a dishevelled and totally dejected look.

There was only one spare table at the back of the café.

It was in a darkened corner and she didn't see the tall figure until it was too late. He was in the booth next to her table, his dark chocolate gaze trained on her.

It was too late to get away.

Far too late.

He got to his feet with the languid grace she'd come to recognise as a sort of physical signature of all of the Ventressi males and came to stand in front of her table.

'Hello, Anna.'

His deep velvet voice stroked along her spine, unravelling a host of memories of a time when her life had held a promise of happiness, a promise that had been snatched away soon after with devastating results.

'Lucio…' *How it hurt to even say his name!*

'May I join you?' He took out the chair opposite and sat down before she even had the chance to refuse, if indeed she'd been able to get her frozen mouth into gear.

'How long has it been?' His eyes ran over her. 'Three? Four years?'

His casual comment completely threw her. She could tell him the exact number of days, almost to the minute, could even recall verbatim his very last angry words to her.

She lifted her chin and met his eyes across the small table. 'I don't remember. It was all such a long time ago.'

'Yes, indeed it was.' He leaned back in his chair and surveyed her flushed features. 'How are you? You look…harried.'

She lowered her gaze to the tablecloth in front of her. 'I'm perfectly fine, thank you.'

The waitress approached and before Anna could open her

mouth Lucio had given her an order—a tall fresh orange juice for herself and a ristretto for him.

Once the waitress had moved away Anna gave him a frowning glance. 'I might have wanted something completely different. You could have at least asked me.'

'Did you want something different?' His expression was indifferent.

'No, but that's not the point.'

'What is the point?'

What, indeed? she thought. There was certainly no point in arguing with him—he was always going to win, no matter what tactics she tried to employ.

She concentrated on the small vase of fresh flowers on the table between them and asked with a casualness she was nowhere near feeling, 'What brings you to Melbourne?'

'I have some business here,' he answered. 'Ventressi Developments has expanded to incorporate the market both here and in Sydney. The property boom has worked in our favour. I thought I'd come over and inspect our assets.'

Her covert glance found his eyes on her and she couldn't help feeling as if he were inspecting her as well.

When the waitress returned with their drinks Anna took the opportunity to inspect his features undetected.

He was still so impossibly handsome, as indeed all the Ventressi males were, even the more unsavoury ones such as his brother, Carlo. But while Carlo was shorter with a tendency to carry excess weight, Lucio was tall and lean, his athletic frame honed to perfection with regular gym sessions. His hair was raven black, his eyes equally so, his jaw almost constantly shadowed and his mouth firm and determined. It was a mouth that could soften—she knew that from experience—but it was also a mouth that could slay one alive and that, too, she knew from bitter experience.

'How long do you expect to be in the country?' she asked, not from any desire to know but more to fill the heavy silence that had fallen between them.

'Three months,' he answered, watching her steadily, 'maybe longer.'

She took a tentative sip of her juice, annoyed to see how her hand shook as she put the glass back down.

'How is your son?'

She almost knocked over the glass at his question. *How did he know she had a son?*

'He's...' She found herself choking on the words. 'He's...not all that well at present.'

'I'm sorry to hear that.'

'Are you?' She lifted her eyes back to his, her expression cynical.

'He's a child,' he responded evenly. 'No child deserves to be unwell. What's the problem?'

It was on the tip of her tongue to tell him the whole story but she bit down on her bottom lip to stop herself from doing so. She reached for her glass once more and took a deep, restorative sip to avoid having to answer.

The silence hung between them awkwardly.

'How old is he?' Lucio asked.

'He's three.'

'Does he ever see his father?'

Her hand tightened momentarily around her frosted glass. 'No.'

'Where is he?'

'Sammy is...with my sister.'

'I meant his father.'

Her eyes went back to his uncertainly. 'I have no idea.'

His indrawn breath sent another chill down her spine.

'Have you even told his father of his existence?' he asked.

'No, but if ever I thought he needed to know I would tell him.' *Not in a hundred lifetimes she wouldn't.* His brother Carlo was the very last person she would tell of Sammy's existence, even if her or, God help them both, Sammy's life depended on it.

'How is your sister, Jenny?' he asked.

Anna was so grateful for the subject change she snatched on to it with both hands. 'Jenny is doing really well. She's finished her first year at university, all High Distinctions.'

'That's quite an achievement,' he commented.

Go on, say it, she thought. *Say how much of an achievement it is for a girl who can't even hear the sound of her own name.* But the embittered words didn't make the distance to her mouth. Instead she schooled her features into an impassive mask and faced him squarely. 'How is your mother?'

'She's very well,' he said. 'Enjoying her grandchildren immensely.'

Anna's stomach instantly hollowed and she couldn't stop herself from asking, 'You have children?'

He shook his head. 'Not me—my sister, Giulia. She has three now.'

Anna remembered his sister with a fondness that time and her present troubles hadn't eradicated. Giulia had been genuinely fond of her and Jenny, making them so welcome at all times.

'I thought you'd be married yourself by now,' she said, staring fixedly at the tiny pearl of an orange seed in the bottom of her glass.

'I don't hold marriage in a great deal of esteem any more.'

She could hardly blame him. He had every right to be cynical after what she'd done.

'I have to go.' She pushed away her empty glass and reached for the bag at her feet.

'No.' One of his hands reached over the table and captured hers.

She felt a jolt of electricity pass through her hand at his touch, her heart thumping behind the wall of her chest as his long fingers curled around hers.

'I want to talk to you a little longer,' he said.

'I have to get back to Sammy,' she said. 'I have a tram to catch and—'

'I'll drive you.'

'No,' she insisted, trying to extricate her hand. 'I live too far away and—'

'Where do you live?'

She wished she could think of an outback town five hundred kilometres away to put him off, but her mind went completely blank.

'Where do you live, Anna?' he repeated.

She lowered her eyes once more and mumbled, 'St Kilda.'

'Hardly what I'd describe as too far away,' he commented wryly.

'It is if you have to walk.'

'You don't have the money for a car or public transport?'

Her chin elevated a fraction. 'I have enough.'

'Do you work?'

'Only a man who has never had a child could ask a question like that,' she said.

He ignored her attempt at sarcasm and added, 'Do you work outside the home?'

'I have two jobs.'

'Quite the career woman then,' he drawled, releasing her hand.

Somehow she had never thought of cleaning hotel rooms and working in a bar as particularly good career moves, but then neither had she envisaged herself as a single mother at twenty-five.

'I enjoy being independent.' She rubbed at her wrist, slanting him a pointed look as she did so.

'I don't remember that being an issue with you in the past.'

How she wished he hadn't mentioned the past!

'I really have to leave...'

'I'd like to talk to you a little longer,' he said. 'Catch up on old times.'

'I have nothing to say.'

He leant back in his chair and surveyed her features for a lengthy moment.

Anna fought against the urge to squirm under his scrutiny but it took a mammoth effort, making her feel almost light-headed and spaced out, as if she were in the middle of a very bad dream. Any minute now she expected to wake up and find herself sitting alone in the café, not staring at the aristocratic features of her ex-fiancé.

'Nothing to say to me after almost four years?' he asked.

'Nothing that springs to mind.'

Something in his dark, unfathomable gaze alerted her to the presence of his simmering anger. She could almost feel it pulsing in the air that separated them; it curled around her, threatening to withdraw the very air from her lungs…

'Excuse me, I have to leave.' She scraped her chair back and got to her feet, relieved he didn't stop her this time.

He rose to his full height and his shadow was cast over her, reminding her of how very tall he was and how very intimidating he could be when he chose to be.

'I'll be seeing you.' He dropped some notes on the table and strode out of the café leaving her standing staring after him. She watched as he went past the café window outside but he didn't turn her way to see if she were looking at him.

He didn't need to, she thought with a little inward shiver—he would have known.

Sammy greeted her with his usual enthusiasm but Anna was almost certain his lips had a bluish tinge which hadn't been there that morning when she'd left.

'Hello, sweetie.' She kissed both his cheeks and then the tip of his button nose. 'Have you been good for Auntie Jenny?'

'I been berry good,' he said. 'I drawed you a picture—see?'

He thrust a picture under her nose and she bent down to inspect it. He'd drawn four stick figures, three of whom she instantly recognised, she could see herself and Jenny and the smallest was, of course, Sammy himself. 'Very nice, but who is this person?' She pointed at the tall figure in the background.

'That's my daddy,' he announced. 'I want one just like Davey's daddy. Can I have one?'

Anna was relieved her three-year-old son was far too young to pick up on her very real distress.

Yes, well, she felt like saying, *Davey's daddy is a mild-mannered ear nose and throat surgeon, not a sleazy opportunist who would lure me into his bed...*

She swallowed the nausea and gave him a wan smile instead. 'I'll have to think about it. Now, why don't we go and see what Auntie Jenny is up to?'

Her sister was in the kitchen, poring over a recipe she hadn't tried before.

Anna tapped her on the shoulder and she swung around with a smile.

'How did the appointment go?' She signed the words with her fingers.

Anna sat down with a defeated sigh and faced her sister, speaking slowly so she could read her lips. 'He needs an operation, an expensive operation.'

'How much?' Jenny asked, the slight distortion of her speech typical of the profoundly deaf, but Anna was used to it and usually understood every word.

She told her the astronomical sum the specialist had estimated and her sister visibly flinched.

'What can we do?'

'I don't know,' Anna said. 'I just don't know.'

'I will get a job!' Jenny signed the words so quickly Anna had trouble following.

'No, what this family needs is a university degree, and you're the one to get it. I'll do some extra shifts on the weekends if you can mind Sammy for me. Somehow we'll get through this…We have to.'

The city hotel where she worked was fully booked over the weekend. The work was arduous and back-breaking but she was determined to raise the necessary funds for Sammy's surgery, even if it meant working herself into the ground in the process.

She stripped the beds in the early check-out rooms first, cleaning the bathrooms and taking in fresh linen and towels. She worked like an automaton, unwilling to allow herself a spare moment in case her thoughts wandered traitorously to Lucio.

Seeing him the day before had unsettled her more than she cared to admit. She hadn't mentioned it to Jenny. A part of her wanted to, but since she hadn't even told her sister the full story behind her break-up with him she didn't see the point in dragging it all up now. It was just too painful.

When their mother had died just two short years after their father's death, Jenny had been completely devastated and had gone into a deep depression. The only thing Anna had been able to think of to bring her out of it was a change of scene, so she had organised a budget overseas holiday, taking in the British Isles and most of Europe.

Even under the tragic circumstances it had been a wonderful holiday and Jenny's spirits had soon picked up, making Anna feel it was worth all the expense.

However when they'd landed in Rome at the tail end of their journey disaster had struck. While she had been trying to book some accommodation at the check-in counter at a cheap hotel, she had left her bag unattended for the briefest moment, thinking Jenny was still beside her. When she had gone to get her purse it was nowhere to be seen; gone too were both their passports, as she'd been carrying all her sister's documentation as well.

The concierge had been more rude than helpful and Anna had soon found herself and a now sobbing Jenny on the street outside with literally nowhere to go.

A tall man was walking along the street carrying a brief-case, the bright summer sunshine picking up the raven silk of his hair. He greeted them both in perfect English although his clear-cut diction suggested it wasn't his native tongue. 'Good afternoon. What seems to be the problem?'

The first thing Anna noticed was how soft his dark eyes looked as they took in Jenny's trembling bottom lip and tear-stained cheeks.

'We've just arrived and my purse has been stolen along with both our passports,' she explained. 'I wonder if you would be so kind as to direct me to the nearest police station.'

'Better still, I'll take you there.' He reached for their two backpacks and lifted them with ease. 'It's only a few blocks, and quicker to walk.'

Anna could well believe it. The traffic was horrendous, even by Melbourne standards, and the constant darting and weaving of motor scooters made it even worse.

She and Jenny fell into step beside the handsome man and for the first time in a very long time she felt safe.

He introduced himself as they walked the next block. 'My name is Lucio Ventressi. My brother Carlo and I run Ventressi Developments. Is this your first visit to Rome?'

'Yes, my sister and I are on our way home to Australia. I'm Anna Stockton, by the way, and this is Jenny.'

He gave them both a heart-stopping smile and formally shook their hands. Anna felt a funny sensation pass through her fingers as soon as his hand touched hers and, feeling embarrassed, withdrew her hand as quickly as she could.

The police report, which would have taken half a day with the phrase book, took only a few minutes with Lucio interpreting for them. Anna was starting to feel more than grateful for his help and seriously wondered what would have happened if he hadn't come along when he had.

He organised the paperwork at the embassy and once that was dealt with took them to a quiet café and bought them both a cool drink.

'I don't know how to thank you,' Anna said. 'You've been so kind.'

He waved away her thanks with a flick of his hand. 'It is no trouble. I have a sister; I know how I would want her to be safe in a foreign country.'

Anna felt her heart increase in size, her cheeks growing warm as his dark gaze meshed with hers.

'Your sister doesn't say much,' he observed a few moments later.

'No,' Anna said. 'Jenny has been deaf since she was two but she can lip-read if you speak slowly. She can speak but she's a little shy around…people she doesn't know.'

'I understand.'

However it was no surprise to find that by the end of the afternoon Jenny had lost her earlier reserve and was quite happily chatting to Lucio, which made the task of refusing his invitation to stay at his family's home all the harder.

'I don't think…'

'You have no accommodation,' he pointed out. 'You'll be adequately chaperoned by both my mother and brother. I would have offered you my own house but it is being redecorated at present. I have been staying with my mother and Carlo to escape the paint fumes.' He gave a wry grimace.

Anna smiled and, turning to Jenny, quickly signed his invitation. Jenny's face broke into a relieved smile, her fragile features instantly losing their pinched look.

'My car is at my office a short distance from here,' Lucio said, leading the way.

Anna caught the tail-end of her sister's excited grin and

lifted her eyebrows in response, a tiny flutter of something indefinable disturbing the lining of her stomach.

Lucio Ventressi was quite easily the most handsome and gallant man she'd ever met. His quiet purposefulness in seeing to the tasks that had to be done had impressed her, so too had his respect for her sister's disability, evidenced by the way he made sure he was facing her when he addressed her so she could read his lips.

Jenny had fallen for his Latin charm as a young girl did, but Anna had felt something much more adult when those chocolate eyes had rested on her.

She'd felt desire.

Anna was finally on to the last of the suites on the luxury presidential floor. Her back was aching and her hair was sticking to her forehead beneath her maid's cap, the tight restriction making her head ache with tension.

She gave the customary short hard knock and called, 'Housekeeping.'

There was no response so, taking the master key, she opened the door and pushed her cleaning trolley in.

It was the largest suite in the hotel, with sweeping views over both the city and Yarra River parklands. The rooms were richly furnished to cater for international tastes, the strong, vibrant colours redolent of the aristocracy or royalty.

She couldn't put her finger on it but something made her uneasy in the apartment.

Maybe it was the obviously disgusting wealth, she ruminated, the opulence of the décor reminding her of how desperately needy she was in comparison.

Or maybe it was the sensation that she was being watched, which was something she'd felt ever since Carlo had shown her the pictures of what had happened between them while she'd been in his bed…

She forced her thoughts away from the pain of the past and tore the sheets off the king-sized bed, bundling them into the laundry hamper before reaching for the clean linen on the bottom of the trolley.

She shook out the sheets and laid them on the bed, straightening the edges and tucking in the corners tightly.

She replaced each of the pillow cases, but stopped on the fourth as she picked up the faint trace of a citrus fragrance that was slightly familiar. She couldn't resist inhaling the scent, its spicy aroma stirring her memories of a time when that very same fragrance had clung to her skin wherever Lucio had caressed her, branding her as his...

She gave herself a mental shake and, turning around, bent down to reach for the bedspread she'd placed on the floor beside the bed.

A pair of Italian-made shoes came into her line of vision, the long legs above them encased in charcoal trousers, the knife-edge seams seeming to go on and on as her eyes slowly travelled upwards.

Her hand fell away from the bedspread as she straightened, shock in every line of her trembling body.

'So we meet again, Anna,' Lucio Ventressi drawled, 'and in my bedroom, too.'

CHAPTER TWO

ANNA stared at him in stupefaction. 'You're…staying *here*?'

His dark eyes moved over her slowly, taking in her maid's black and white uniform before coming back to her troubled gaze. 'As you see.'

'I…I won't be long.' She bent to retrieve the bedspread but he moved one leather-clad foot and stepped on it to prevent her from lifting it.

'Leave it.'

'I have to finish the room.' She gave the bedspread another little useless tug.

'I said *leave it*.'

She let the bedspread go and straightened, unconsciously wiping her damp palms on her white apron.

He was angry.

Unmistakably angry.

His dark eyes positively glittered with it as they bored down into hers. 'What the hell are you doing, cleaning rooms in a hotel?' he asked.

Her chin went up in fierce pride. 'Someone has to do it.'

'You said you had two jobs. What's the other one?'

Her chin went a fraction higher. 'I work in a bar.'

He sucked in a furious breath and swore vehemently, 'Whatever for?'

'The usual reason—money.'

'You are poor?' He frowned down at her.

'Compared to someone like you, yes.'

'Don't play with words,' he growled. 'Answer me. Are you having financial difficulties?'

19

She wished she didn't have to admit it but a sudden vision of little Sammy came into her head and her stomach caved in with fear at the thought of losing him for the sake of her pride.

She lowered her eyes from the heat of his. 'Yes.'

'What sort of difficulties?' His tone was now surprisingly gentle.

'Sammy needs…an operation,' she said. 'I don't have private insurance but if I wait until it's his turn on the public waiting list…it might be too late.'

'What's wrong with him?'

'He has a heart condition.'

'Serious?'

She took a painful breath. 'He needs the surgery to survive into adulthood.'

He swore again. 'How much is this…operation?' he asked after a short pause.

She told him and he didn't even flinch, which somehow annoyed her. It was such a pittance to someone like him, pin money really, and yet it could save a child's life.

Her child's life.

She watched him out of the corner of her eye. He was thinking…no—calculating…planning.

'I might be able to help you,' he said after another one of his strategically timed pauses.

'Why would you want to do that?' Suspicion crept into her tone as she lifted her eyes back to his.

'I have my reasons.' His expression gave nothing away.

'A loan, you mean?'

'No.'

'No?'

He shook his head. 'No.'

'What, then?' Her stomach tightened.

'I will pay for Sammy's health care, but I have some conditions on the deal.'

'Conditions?' She swallowed the restriction in her throat. 'What sort of conditions?'

His eyes held hers determinedly. 'You can save your son's life but you must agree to do something for me in return.'

'I will do anything to save my son's life,' she said. 'Anything.'

The corner of his hard mouth lifted in a slight smile. 'I'm very glad to hear that as I was expecting much more resistance on your part.'

The fingertips of fear tickled along her spine. 'What do you want me to do?'

He gave her another contemplative look. 'I thought you would have guessed by now, *cara*.'

Something in his expression made her stomach turn over unexpectedly.

'I have no idea what you want from me,' she said, even as her fear crept up another notch.

'Do you not?'

'I'm afraid I have very little experience in decoding other people's motives.'

'Ah, but you're very experienced in other matters, are you not?'

She refused to allow him the satisfaction of seeing how much his cruel taunt hurt her. 'I have enough experience to know that what you are offering is not a simple act of charity,' she said.

'How very insightful of you, Anna.'

'Get it over with.' She drew in a ragged breath. 'What form of torture have you got planned for me?'

'Torture?' One aristocratic brow rose expressively. 'Now there's a word I like.'

'Don't play games with me,' she bit out. 'Tell me what it is you want.'

He watched the play of emotion on her face for endless

moments. Anna wished she had the courage to storm out, throwing his offer in his face without even hearing his conditions but this wasn't a battle she was fighting for herself. This was Sammy's battle and it was for his life.

'Please, Lucio—' she was so close to begging it sickened her '—don't make this any harder than it is.'

'You find it hard to deal with me?' he asked.

I find it hard to look at you, she wanted to say. *I find it hard to think of all I've lost, all I could have had if…*

'You're not making this easy.'

'And why should I?' he asked, his tone hardening. 'You ripped my heart from my chest.'

'I…I didn't mean to…'

'*Dio!* You slept with my brother!'

How could she deny it? Carlo had photos to prove it, even if she could barely remember what had happened.

'Is Sammy his child?' he asked.

She felt as if someone had given her a king-hit.

Each and every time she and Lucio had made love he'd used a condom. He'd been insistent, wanting to protect her, claiming there was plenty of time to start a family once they were married…

'I…I think so.'

He swore again but even in Italian it was unprintable. 'You disgust me. You spread your legs for him even while our wedding was days away.'

'I'm sorry…'

'You will be when I've finished with you.'

'Wh…what do you mean?'

His eyes burned as they came back to hers, the line of his normally firm mouth now so tight it hinted at cruelty.

'I will pay for my nephew's surgery but in exchange I want you back in my bed.'

Her eyes widened in alarm. '*No!*'

'No?' The eyebrow rose once more. 'I didn't think that was a word you were accustomed to using a great deal.'

She closed her eyes so she didn't have to see his derision. 'I can't do it.'

'All right.' He dismissed her with a step away. 'Finish the room and get out.'

He was halfway out of the door when she came to her senses. This was about Sammy, not her.

'Lucio…'

'Yes?' He turned to face her, his expression one of extreme boredom.

She found it hard to hold his gaze and lowered her eyes to the floor at his feet, the collapse of her pride making her shoulders slump in defeat.

'I'll do it,' she said hollowly. 'I'll do what you ask.'

'Good.' He folded his arms across his chest, his manner so casual she thought they might as well have been discussing a dinner engagement instead of something as life-changing as resuming a relationship that would only hurt her all over again in the end. 'Come out into the lounge and we will discuss the details more fully.'

Anna followed him out of the bedroom, unable to stop herself from thinking how ironic it was. She'd just made his bed, now he wanted her to lie on it—with him.

He moved across to the well-appointed bar. 'Would you like a drink?'

'I don't drink.' *Any more*, she wanted to tack on, but didn't. She'd taken her last drink in the company of his brother and it had taught her the lesson of a lifetime.

She watched as he poured soda water in a glass, adding a decent measure of Scotch to his but leaving hers plain.

'Ice?'

She shook her head and took the glass with an unsteady hand.

'What's the matter, *cara*?' His tone was teasing. 'Does the thought of sharing my bed once more unsettle you?'

'I can't say I'm looking forward to it.'

He had the audacity to laugh. 'Ah, but I am looking forward to it enough for both of us.'

Her belly crawled with sudden desire, making her feel hot all over.

'This is nothing more than prostitution,' she sniped at him.

'Not prostitution—retribution,' he corrected. 'For past sins.'

'I'm sure you would've more than made up for my "past sins" by now,' she bit out.

'If you mean by that I have had many other women, then yes, I have.'

She wished she hadn't spoken. It hurt her too much to think of him with someone else—a hundred someone elses.

'But then, no doubt, you've been having your fun as well,' he said. 'Someone with your…needs cannot go without for too long.'

She felt her face flame with colour as she remembered the needs he'd awakened in her. She'd been a willing student to passion, her innocence no barrier to the ecstasy she'd experienced in his arms.

'I'm a mother now.'

'I find motherhood very sexy.' His eyes moved over her full breasts. 'Very sexy indeed.'

She turned away from his probing gaze and addressed the sofa in front of her. 'For how long do you wish to conduct this…arrangement?'

'Not long.'

She turned at that, unable to disguise the relief in her expression. 'How long?'

He gave her a knowing smile, 'I can see how your mind is working but I'm not going to let you off that easily.'

'I didn't think you would.' Her tone was deliberately dry.

'I will be in Melbourne for a period of three months,' he said. 'During that time I wish for you to be my mistress.'

Anna felt her stomach hit the floor and bounce back up again.

'By that I mean you will live with me and satisfy any needs I have.'

She was all too familiar with those needs!

'But what about Sammy and Jenny?' she asked, searching desperately for a way out. 'I can't move in with you and leave them.'

'I have leased a large property in South Yarra; it will be available in a couple of days. Your sister and son shall join us there until such time as I cease to...' he hesitated slightly over the word, drawing out her pain '...need you.'

'Moving house can be very unsettling for a child...'

'So, I imagine, is dying.'

She blenched at the blunt cruelty of his statement. 'How can you do this?' She glared at him. 'You're bargaining with a child's life!'

He stepped towards her and, grasping her upper arms, pulled her against him, his eyes spitting fire at her as he ground out, 'He could have been my child but you denied me that privilege. Do you know the hell I have been through, thinking of the way you seduced my brother in my absence? *Do you?*'

She squeezed her eyes shut against the bitterness of his tone.

'I have died a thousand deaths to think of you with him. I have heard your cries of pleasure in my dreams, cries of pleasure that belonged to me.'

'Don't...' She tried to escape his iron hold. 'Let me go!'

'No.' He hauled her even closer, his chest now pressing against her breasts, reawakening a host of memories in her.

'Don't tell me "don't" when you said yes to Carlo. You will say yes to me and mean it.'

'No.'

'I will not take no.'

'I don't want you.'

'I can make you want me,' he stated with a confidence that terrified her.

'Please don't ask this of me.'

'I'm not asking you—I'm telling you. You will be mine for the period of three months; otherwise your son will not receive the help he needs.'

She wanted to call his bluff, how she wanted to! Sammy was his nephew, he knew that now. How could he turn his back on his own flesh and blood if she refused to do as he asked?

He would turn his back as his pride would not allow him to do otherwise. Her betrayal had destroyed his feelings for her and now his only motivation was revenge.

She could hardly blame him.

What she had done, albeit inadvertently, had been unforgivable. She'd slept with his brother and, if Carlo's detestable photographs were any indication, she had enjoyed each and every damning minute.

She bowed her head in defeat, her voice empty as she asked, 'When do you want me to…start?'

'I want you to start now.'

Her head snapped back and her wide eyes met his. *'Now?'*

'Why not now?' he asked with implacable calm. 'We are here and we are alone.'

She had to think on her feet. 'I'm supposed to be working.'

'Your job ended ten minutes ago.'

'I can't afford not to work!' she protested.

'Did I forget to mention?' His lip curled. 'I will pay you for your…services.'

Her shame knew no bounds. Hot colour went from her head to her feet and back again. 'You can't do this to me.'

'I can and I will,' he said.

'Do you hate me this much?'

His dark eyes bored into hers. 'Suffice it to say I have waited a long time for this moment.'

'You're so bitter…'

'Does that surprise you?'

'No, but…I would've thought you would've forgotten by now. I was just a fleeting episode in your life.'

'You were my life!' he ground out. 'I wanted to give you the world but you threw it in my face.'

There was nothing she could say in her defence. 'I'm sorry…'

'I don't want your apology.' His harshly delivered words cut the air like a knife.

'What do you want?' She raised her agonised features to his. 'Do you want me to beg?'

'No,' he said heavily. 'I want you to feel what I felt when I looked at you. I want you to writhe with desire for me the way I did when I saw you.'

His words totally shocked her. 'Lucio, this is all wrong…Surely you can see that?'

'No.' His hands were like twin vices on her upper arms. 'I want you on any terms. You can either come to me out of gratitude or out of hate; I am indifferent. I will have you no matter what you feel.'

She opened her mouth to protest but it was too late. His head came down and his mouth crashed against hers, her senses reeling at the feel of his lips on hers once more.

His tongue drove through the trembling shield of her lips, drawing from her a response she didn't want to give but couldn't stop herself from giving. With his first branding kiss she was transported back four years to a time when he had only to look at her for her to squirm with red-hot desire.

She felt his hand searching for her breast and leaned into him to give him the access he craved, her limbs loosening when his thumb found her nipple, the tantalising touch so exquisite she felt as if she were floating on a sea of need, each great wave threatening to consume her.

She felt the wall at her back, his hard body at her front, the heated trajectory of his desire so arrantly male against her she had trouble establishing where he ended and she began.

She fought against her response, unwilling to communicate her need but unable to control it. Her body craved the domination of his, each and every nerve singing with delight as his hands moved over her, shaping her, caressing her…subduing her.

His mouth moved from hers to the upper curve of her breasts, his nimble fingers freeing them from the tight restraint of her uniform, his hungry eyes consuming her in heated anticipation.

'You are so beautiful,' he groaned as he bent his mouth to one pert bud. 'I have dreamt of this moment…ached for this…'

His words both thrilled and terrified her. She wanted him but there was the issue of his brother lying between them. She had no memory of what had occurred in Carlo's bed but she knew it had resulted in a child—her child. How could she go from his brother's arms to his without calling her morals into account?

'Lucio…' She pushed against his chest with a will she hardly recognised as her own.

'What?' His one word was sharp.

'I don't know if I can do this.'

'You baulk at sharing my bed after sharing my brother's?'

She flinched at his harsh tone. 'This has nothing to do with…Carlo; this is about you and…me.'

'It has everything to do with Carlo,' he said. 'You had his child. You rejected me for him.'

'I did not reject you for him,' she countered. 'I left you both.'

'Is that supposed to be some consolation?'

'No, but I thought—'

'You thought!' he spat in derision. 'When, pray tell, did you think? You seduced my brother, thinking you would get away with it because I was out of town, but you seriously underestimated Carlo.'

Oh, how she had underestimated him!

'Carlo saw through your innocent façade,' he said. 'I, on the other hand, was blinded by love.'

'You never loved me,' she said in a hollow tone.

'I loved you with every fibre of my being. You destroyed that love by enticing Carlo when his guard was down.'

She stared at him incredulously. 'Is that what he told you?'

He met her look with steely eyes. 'I know my brother would never betray me willingly.'

She wasn't sure how to answer such a statement. Carlo had planned his seduction so well even she hadn't seen it coming.

'Your loyalty to your brother is admirable but I would've thought you might have spared a thought for what we had shared.'

'It's a pity you didn't do likewise when you bribed my brother into your bed.'

'What?'

'Wasn't that your goal?' he asked.

'I don't know what you mean…'

'Oh, come on, Anna.' His tone was scathing. 'Surely you don't expect me to spell it out for you? Carlo and I are joint inheritors of the Ventressi Corporation. On the birth of an heir, a lump sum will be allocated to the child when he turns twenty-one.'

'An heir?' She stared at him blankly.

'Your son is your ticket to wealth,' he said. 'As a Ventressi he stands to inherit a veritable fortune. Why haven't you told Carlo the good news?'

She felt sick to her stomach.

'You have denied him his child for three years,' he said. 'Don't you think it's time you told him?'

She inspected her nail-bitten hands. 'I didn't see the need to.'

'No—' his breath came out forcibly '—you wouldn't.' You'd rather bide your time and wait for the moment when revenge would be sweetest.'

'What?'

'Don't play the innocent with me,' he snarled at her. 'Carlo is married with a child on the way. What were you hoping for? To step in now and announce Sammy's existence?'

Anna stared at him without speaking.

'I can see how your mind works,' he continued. 'You have needs that need to be met. What better way than presenting Carlo with a child he had no idea existed so you could twist the screws.'

She was so totally gob-smacked by his revelation she could barely think.

Carlo? Married? A child on the way?

'I had no intention of ever telling Carlo,' she said through bone-white lips.

'No?' His look was sceptical. 'Don't play me for a fool, Anna. I've seen how women like you work. Blackmail is second nature to get what you want, but think again if you imagine you'll succeed in hauling yourself a fortune. I won't allow it.'

'I don't want anything to do with Carlo,' she insisted.

'Good, because from now on you'll be dealing exclusively with me.'

The burning heat of his gaze scorched her wherever it touched her, making her aware of her body in a way she hadn't been for such a long time. She felt the stirring of her breasts, their weight increasing, and the tightening of her nipples, aching for his touch. Her mouth felt sensitive, her lips swollen by his savage kiss, and she realised with a sickening arrow of shame that she wanted him.

'Where are your normal clothes?' he asked bluntly.

'In my locker in the staff room.'

'Go and get changed and be back here in ten minutes,' he instructed her. 'I will speak to your employer and inform him of your new position with me.'

Her face drained of all colour as she stood uncertainly before him. 'You're going to tell him I'm to be *your mistress*?'

He gave a careless shrug. 'Why shouldn't I? It's the truth, is it not?'

'Can't you tell him I'm your secretary or something? Anything would be preferable to...'

'You will not only be my mistress, Anna, you will give every outward appearance of enjoying it, do you understand?'

She threw him a resentful glance. 'What about Jenny and Sammy? What am I supposed to tell them?'

He looked at her for a long moment before speaking. 'Sammy is too young to understand. Your sister, however, need only be told we are resuming our relationship indefinitely.'

'Indefinitely?' The word flew from her startled mouth. 'But you said it was only to be for three months!'

His eyes glinted with dark purpose. 'I'm the one calling the shots here, Anna. You'd do very well to remember.'

She swung from the apartment with her fury around her like an aura as she stomped towards the service lift. She stabbed at the call button as if it were a part of his hateful anatomy instead, hatred seething within her until she was sure she would explode with it.

What trick of fate had led her to that café?

What force was at work to make her path cross with his after all these years?

The first time she'd met him he'd offered her help, but back then his help had come without a price tag. He'd taken her and Jenny to his mother's house, where they were made to feel very welcome in spite of the language barrier.

Her thoughts drifted back to that time, a deep pang of regret assailing her at how things had gone from such happiness to such despair so quickly.

Lucio's mother had been an elegant, diminutive woman, her natural grace and charm making the girls feel at home right from the start. Anna's earlier intention of leaving within the week was put back at the Ventressis' insistence. They wanted to show her and Jenny more of Rome and the outlying sights of interest.

So Anna had extended their visit and they'd spent glorious summer days visiting Naples and Pompeii and the Amalfi coast.

A trip had been planned to Tivoli, thirty-one kilometres northeast of Rome, but on the morning of their departure Jenny had announced she was unwell with a headache so Jovanna, Lucio's mother, had insisted on staying home with her to look after her. Carlo had still been away on business, so it had been just Lucio and Anna who drove the short distance to Villa d'Este.

She had barely contained her excitement at the thought of a day in his company. Her awareness of him had grown continuously over the past two weeks, her heart tripping over itself every time his dark gaze slid to hers across the dinner table or across the room.

She was too inexperienced to know for sure if he were interested in her, but she liked the way he listened to her when she told him something of interest, his dark eyes warm with amusement as they rested on her up-tilted face.

'You like our country, Anna?' he asked as he drove towards the Benedictine convent.

'I love your country,' she answered, glancing at him shyly. 'I love everything—the food, the wine, the climate…'

'And the people?' His dark brow lifted expressively.

'I adore the people.' She turned back to face the front of the car, her cheeks suddenly warm.

His soft rumble of laughter sent delicious shivers along the entire length of her spine and she had to press her knees together to stop the rush of warmth from her lower body. She felt his glance but didn't look his way.

'There is so much I want to show you, Anna.' He drew the car to a halt and smiled across at her.

She smiled back, her heart swelling in her chest at the warmth of his gaze.

'You don't mind it's just us today?' she asked as he helped her out of the car.

His eyes flicked to the soft curve of her mouth before coming back to her shining gaze.

'I adore the fact that we are finally alone,' he said and lowered his mouth to hers.

Anna was lost from that moment. His kiss was exquisitely gentle, drawing from her a response she had no control over. She had been kissed occasionally in the past but nothing came close to the feel of Lucio's mouth on hers. His lips were firm and dry, his tongue when it entered her mouth determined but controlled, as if he were aware of her limited experience.

Later, all Anna could remember of the Villa d'Este was

the sound of water running in the background and the chirruping birds in the terraced gardens interspersed with the distant tolling of bells. She was lost in the dreamy sensation of walking arm in arm with Lucio, hardly even taking in what he told her about the villa.

'This estate was established by Cardinal Ippolito d'Este, son of Lucrezia Borgia. The terraced gardens and fountains were laid out by Liggorio and Giacomo della Porta,' he informed her. 'See this avenue here?' He pointed ahead of them. 'This is the Terrace of One Hundred Fountains.'

Anna's gaze swept over the moss-encased shapes of eagles, ships, grotesques and obelisks with eyes shining with love, not interest.

She was in love with Lucio.

'You are not listening, *cara*,' he chided her gently.

She tilted her head at him. 'Yes I am, test me.'

'All right.' He pushed up her chin with one finger. 'Tell me how many fountains are in the Viale delle Cento Fontane.'

She ran her tongue over the sensitive surface of her lips and smiled up at him vacantly. 'I give up. How many?'

'*Dio*,' he growled playfully, pulling her back into his arms. 'What am I going to do with such an inattentive tourist?'

She laughed at the mock severity of his tone. 'I would be more attentive if you hadn't completely distracted me by kissing me as soon as we arrived.'

'I wanted to kiss you.' He stared at her smiling mouth. 'I have been dreaming of doing so from the first time I saw you comforting your sister on the street.'

'Have you really?'

'Have you not seen the way I cannot take my eyes off you?' he asked. 'How my fingers long to touch you and my body to claim you?'

She felt the growing heat of his lower body against the

softness of hers, felt too the leap of her own pulses in response to his nearness.

'I…I'm not used to feeling like this,' she confessed shyly.

'You are inexperienced, *cara*?' he asked gently.

She found it hard to hold the intensity of his gaze. 'I'm sorry.'

'Sorry?' he gasped. 'Do not be sorry! Do you realise how I have longed to meet someone like you? Someone who hasn't slept with dozens of men before me?'

'That's rather an old-fashioned view, Lucio,' she couldn't help pointing out.

He laughed. 'Yes, I know, but I am an Italian so I am allowed to be traditional in my views, yes?'

'If you're really an Italian traditionalist you must have some Italian maiden already picked out for your partner in life.'

'I will choose my own wife,' he said. 'And I have decided she will be you.'

'Me?' she squeaked.

'Why not you?' He glinted down at her. 'I am besotted with you. I want you so much my body aches with it.'

'But I'm only twenty-one,' she said.

'So? I am thirty, only nine years older.'

'But I'm Australian.'

'So?'

'I should go home—I've got a job to go back to and—'

'As my wife you will be able to travel the world, your sister too. I will not tie you to my country. I have some interests in Australia anyway, some members of my family emigrated years ago. We could live between both countries.'

'Oh, Lucio.' She sank into his arms. 'I can't believe this is happening to me.'

'Believe it, *cara*,' he whispered into her hair. 'This was meant to be. It is fate.'

*   *   *

Fate.

Anna got out of the lift and made her way to the staff room, her heart sinking at what she'd just committed herself to.

Three months as Lucio's lover—no, mistress, she corrected herself. Mistress seemed to suggest a relationship of lesser value. She would be dispensed with as soon as he tired of her, his revenge complete.

It was understandable that he was still angry. She knew it was unreasonable of her to expect any different. In the same place she would have been devastated. It still hurt even now to think of him with someone else in the way they had loved, their bodies so attuned to each other he had only to look at her to make her want him.

She stepped out of her maid's uniform and back into her street clothes, not for the first time wishing they weren't quite so old and unfashionable.

She shook out her hair and lamented the absence of make-up on her pale face, wishing she could have some sort of physical armour against Lucio's threats.

He'd changed.

He was no longer the gentle, gallant man of her dreams. He was a dark avenger, intent on righting the wrongs of the past by making her pay the price for her sins.

Oh, how she had paid for those sins!

A day never closed without her trying to make sense of her totally uncharacteristic actions. If the photographs didn't exist to tell her otherwise she would have sworn it was all a lie.

On the surface Carlo had always presented himself as the charming younger brother of Lucio, happy to be the second in command. He'd taken the news of his brother's engagement with his usual equanimity but somehow Anna had suspected he was annoyed. She'd often found his eyes on her at unexpected moments, his narrow-eyed look unsettling her. She'd wanted to speak to Lucio about it but he was tying up some loose business ends so he could concentrate on their wedding, which was set for one month's time.

Those early weeks had flown past in a haze of sensual delight as Lucio had taught her the language of love and schooled her body into speaking it fluently. She had cried out her pleasure, sobbed in his arms at the intensity of her feelings, as he'd held her close, his long limbs entwined with hers.

Her happiness had known no bounds. She'd been glowing with it; her steps, so laden before with grief and tribulation, now light and carefree.

Even Jenny had lost her fragile look, her thin fifteen-year-old body filling out at last, her confidence visibly growing.

Together they had planned Anna's wedding, staying up late at night going over designs and flowers, neither of them mentioning their mother, but both wishing she could have seen how happily everything had turned out.

But it hadn't turned out happily.

Carlo had seen to that.

He had handed her a glass of champagne on one of the first evenings Lucio had been away on business, his smile a perfect guise for what he had in store.

'To your future, Anna.' He lifted his own glass.

Something in his tone alerted her to a sense of danger, but she ignored it, comforting herself with the knowledge that Jenny was in the next room.

It was only later, when she finally woke up in Carlo's bed, the brilliant sunlight like an accusing eye on her naked form, that she realised her mistake.

Even if she had cried out no one would have heard her.

CHAPTER THREE

ANNA forced her thoughts away from the past.

It couldn't change anything. What she had done could not be undone. She'd slept with her fiancé's brother and there was evidence to prove it. Even though she could scratch together some vague details of that night, most of it still remained a blur.

She had no choice but to believe what Carlo had told Lucio.

She had seduced his brother and when he'd woken and realised his mistake he had taken the photographs to prove how wanton she was, knowing he'd never be able to convince Lucio without solid evidence.

As evidence went it was as damning as ever could be. She still cringed with shame at the way her body had been sprawled on that bed, her breasts and femininity on full show like something out of a B-grade porn film.

And out of seduction Sammy had been conceived, which had intensified the torture one hundredfold.

He was an innocent child; how could she ever tell him the circumstances of his conception?

She took a deep breath and lifted her hand to knock on the penthouse door, but before her knuckles connected the door sprang open and she almost fell into the room.

'What took you so long?' Lucio growled down at her.

'I've only been ten minutes or so,' she said somewhat defensively.

'I said ten minutes, not ten or so.' He slammed the door behind her, making his statement sound all the more commanding.

She sucked in an angry breath. So this was the way he wanted to play it, was it? I'm the master, you are the slave.

Resentment burned in her blue eyes as she faced him. 'I had to hand in my locker key.'

'When I designate a time I expect you to obey it to the second.'

'Is there anything else?' She glared at him. 'Sir?'

His jaw tightened, 'As a matter of fact—yes.'

Something in his expression sent a shiver of apprehension right through her. There was an unmistakable edge of cold-bloodedness about the firm line of his mouth, as if he were intent on making her suffer as much as possible for what she had done to him.

'Get undressed.'

She reared back in shock. '*What?*'

'You heard.'

She gaped at him for what seemed like an eternity, her heart hammering inside her, making her feel faint.

'You can't be serious!'

'Get undressed or I will do it for you.' The ruthlessness of his tone shocked her; it was so at variance with the man she had once known as a passionate but respectful lover.

'I…I need time…'

'You've had four years.'

Her eyes flew back to his. 'Why are you doing this?'

'You know why,' he said.

'Isn't this taking revenge a little too far?' Her composure was beginning to crack around the edges but she did her best to conceal it from him.

'I have thought about this moment for a long time. You did this for my brother; now you will do it for me.'

A bubble of hysteria spilled into her throat and she swallowed deeply to stop it escaping.

'Don't do this, Lucio.' Her voice was a mere whisper, her tone now pleading.

'Do not tell me what I can or can't do!' His words were as sharp as a whip cracking. 'You will do as I say or bear the consequences.'

'I will hate you for ever.'

'You showed me your hatred by sleeping with my brother. Now it is time for me to demonstrate my own.'

She stood immobile, coldness creeping into her bones even though the temperature outside was in the high twenties.

Never in her worst nightmares had she ever expected to be in such a situation. Her worries over Sammy, her fears for his health on top of seeing Lucio again, were suddenly all too much.

In spite of years of feminist teachings that insisted she take control and not give in to feminine weakness, she did what any self-respecting girl would do.

She burst into floods of tears.

Lucio stood in a frozen silence, the sight of Anna's shaking shoulders and bent golden head driving all thought of revenge out of his mind.

'Anna.' He lowered his voice and stepped towards her. 'Anna…'

She lifted her streaming face to glare at him. 'Now see what you've done. Are you happy now?'

His throat moved up and down in a swallow and one of his hands raked through the thickness of his hair in a distracted manner.

'I didn't mean to make you cry.'

'D…didn't you?' she sobbed. 'What did you mean to do, then?'

He drew in a ragged breath. 'I'm sorry. I had temporarily forgotten the stress you must be under with your little son.'

His gentle tone only made her cry all the more. 'It's been so…so hard,' she choked. 'I've done all I can do but it's not enough. I can't see him…die…Surely you understand that?'

His dark eyes held hers. 'Of course I understand that.'

She sniffed and he handed her a clean white handkerchief. She buried her face in it, glad of a chance to escape his probing, watchful gaze.

'I will take you home to him.'

'I can catch a tram.'

'Anna.' His hands came to rest on the top of her shoulders, leaving her no choice but to lift her gaze to his. 'This…thing between us is between *us*. I want you to know I will not involve either Sammy or Jenny.'

'How very decent of you.' Her tone was laced with sarcasm as she removed herself from his hold.

'You are overwrought.'

'I am angry!' she shot back. 'How can you humiliate me in such a way?'

'So now you've had your little cry you are back to spitting and snarling at me, eh, *cara*?'

'I would like to scratch your damn eyes out,' she said through clenched teeth. 'I hate you.'

'I am unconcerned about your feelings for me,' he responded with implacable calm. 'By the time our affair is over you will undoubtedly hate me a whole lot more.'

The breath she drew in hurt her all the way down into her lungs.

'How can you live with yourself? How can you stand there and speak so calmly of what amounts to nothing more than exploitation?'

'I am not exploiting you, *cara*, I am helping you.'

'For your own ends, yes!'

His eyes sent her a warning. 'I will not tolerate your insults. I suggest you get them over with while I am still feeling sorry for you, for I can assure you I will not be so gracious in future.'

She swung away from him in fury, stomping across the room to put as much distance as she could between them.

'When do I have to report for…duty?' She made it sound as distasteful as she could, hoping to annoy him.

'I will give you two days to pack your things. I will send a car for you all on Tuesday.'

'Just like that?'

He gave her an unreadable look. 'Just like that.'

Anna sat in miserable silence on the journey back to her flat, the tall, forbidding figure behind the wheel not even once glancing her way.

She gave him some clipped directions and he turned the Maserati into the kerb outside her run-down flat.

'Thank you for the ride home,' she mumbled and made to get out of the car.

'Wait.' His hand came down on her arm, stalling her.

Her eyes went to the steel bracelet of his tanned fingers around her wrist before travelling back to his dark, unfathomable eyes.

'Aren't you going to introduce me to your son?' His expression held a trace of mockery.

'He's probably asleep.' She reached for the door again but his hold tightened warningly.

'Then you will wake him and introduce his uncle to him.'

'I will do no such thing!'

'Mummee!' a little voice called from the top floor of the flat. 'Mummee!'

Anna stumbled from the car, hardly even noticing how Lucio's hand had fallen away from hers as if she had burnt him.

'Hello, darling.' She waved one still shaking hand towards her little son's smiling face.

'Who's dat man?' he asked.

'He's…'

'Tell him I'm his uncle,' Lucio said from behind her.

Anna swung back around to face him. 'I can't do that!'

His expression hardened as he looked down at her. 'Why not?'

She shifted her tortured gaze away from the heat of his. 'Because I told Jenny that Sammy was your son.'

'*Dio!*'

'I had to,' she continued. 'I didn't want to upset her by...I thought it the best thing.'

'So you weren't even honest with your sister over what you had done?'

She bit her lip and turned away.

'We will discuss this later,' he said and took her hand once more.

Jenny's startled expression spoke volumes as Anna and Lucio entered the flat. Her fingers flew with rapid-fire questions, her elfin face troubled.

'It's all right,' Anna said, signing and speaking at the same time. 'Lucio and I are seeing each other again.'

Jenny's face broke into a smile and she spoke out loud, 'Really?'

'Yes, Jenny,' Lucio said. 'It is true. We are resuming our relationship. Our...misunderstanding has been dealt with and we are now planning our future.'

'I am so happy for you!' Jenny threw her hands to the sides of her face in rapturous delight. 'I have dreamed of this day!'

Anna quickly signed back, 'Don't get too excited, Jen. We're not getting married—just living together. He wants us all to live with him.'

Jenny's smile hardly wavered as she signed back, 'What does that matter? The important thing is that you are together once more. Sammy will have his father with him at last.'

Oh, the tangled web, Anna thought. It was as if every lie she'd ever told was coming back to haunt her.

She hadn't thought she'd ever see Lucio again, so telling her sister he was the father of her son had seemed the right thing to do at the time. She hadn't realised she was even pregnant until she was well into her third month, having put down her disrupted pattern to the trauma she'd gone through with her break-up with Lucio and her guilt over how she'd torn their lives apart.

'I can see I shall have to learn to sign or you two will be saying things behind my back without me knowing it,' Lucio drawled.

Jenny giggled.

Anna seethed.

And Sammy came bolting into the room, coming to a complete stop in front of the tall figure standing next to his mother.

'Who are you?' he asked as he hadn't received an answer earlier.

Lucio squatted down and held out his hand, 'I am your father.'

'Are you really?' Sammy's deep brown eyes widened.

'I am indeed,' he said, lifting the small child up into his arms.

Seeing them together for the first time made Anna's heart squeeze painfully. No one would ever know they weren't father and son. They had the same raven hair and chocolate eyes, the same determined chin and intractable mouth.

'I have heard you have not been well,' Lucio said. 'But I am here now so you can concentrate on getting better.'

'But what about when I get better?' Sammy asked. 'Will you still be here den?'

Anna turned away, unable to watch him lie to her child.

'I will make you a promise, Sammy,' he said. 'You get better and I will make sure I see you every day.'

A tide of fear rose in her stomach as realisation dawned.

The Ventressis were a wealthy family with access to the best legal advice money could buy. It would be a simple task to whisk Sammy away from his hard-pressed single mother and return him to his wealthy father. Carlo would be able to give him the sorts of things she had only ever dreamed about. The best health care, a private education and holidays by the seaside—the list went on and on inside her head. She wouldn't have a legal leg to stand on. She had withheld the news of his birth from his father, which would, no doubt, be viewed in a pretty poor light in a country as patriarchal as Italy.

'Sammy—' Anna's voice came out croakily '—why don't you and Auntie Jenny go to the shops for me while I discuss some things with...your father?' She sent her sister a grateful glance as Jenny took his hand.

'Come on, Sammy,' Jenny said. 'We can take a detour to the park on the way.'

'Goodie!'

Anna waited until the front door had closed behind them before turning to Lucio. 'You had no right to lie to him like that.'

He held her fiery look with ease. 'I wasn't lying to him. I meant it. I will see him every day.'

'For how long? Three months? He's a little child, Lucio, not a toy you can pick up and put down whenever the fancy takes you. He'll become attached to you and then when you leave he'll...'

'He is most definitely a Ventressi,' he said, ignoring her tirade. 'But he looks more like me than Carlo.'

'Well, thank God he doesn't have your personality,' she shot back before she could stop herself.

He stood watching her for a long moment, his closed expression leaving her confused at what was going on behind the dark screen of his contemplative gaze.

'He should have been mine.' He broke the heavy silence.

She looked down at her hands, 'We can't change the past, no matter how much we might want to.'

'So you regret your actions?'

'I'm surprised you can ask that,' she said. 'I regret everything. I regret meeting you and falling in love with you—'

'You did not love me!' His fierce tone cut her off. 'You wanted a meal ticket and you reeled me in with your fake innocence. I was a fool to fall for it. You were a cheap little tramp who had her sights set on Carlo from the first.'

'That's not true!'

'Isn't it?' His dark eyes narrowed. 'He told me how you pursued him.'

'*What?*'

'All the time I wasn't there he said he had to fend off your advances.'

'That's a lie!'

He gave her a scathing look. 'You think I would hold your word over that of my brother?'

'No, but that doesn't mean he's telling the truth.'

'He's never lied to me before or indeed since. But you— your whole life is a lie. You have kept my family ignorant of your son's existence.'

'But you seemed to know about him, all the same,' she pointed out. 'You asked after him yesterday in the café, remember?'

'Do you think I wouldn't make it my business to know everything about you?'

Fear clawed its way back up her spine. 'What do you mean?'

He gave her an imperious look down the length of his aristocratic nose. 'I had you investigated. You had only to sneeze and I heard about it.'

'*No!*'

'Yes, *cara*.' He gave a self-satisfied smile. 'I have been watching you for four years.'

'Why wait until now to approach me?'

He gave a casual shrug of one broad shoulder. 'Tactics; *cara*. I wanted to make sure you wouldn't refuse my offer.'

'Your blackmail, you mean!'

'Blackmail is such an unpleasant term.' He inspected his nails for a moment. 'I'm doing you a favour and you are paying me back in kind.'

'I can't believe I'm hearing this.' She crossed her arms and glared at him.

'You are finding the terms of our agreement a little distasteful?'

'I'm finding them nauseating!'

'No doubt you will soon come to realise which side your bread is buttered and adjust your opinions accordingly.'

She wanted to scream with frustration. She felt so totally impotent; she had nowhere to turn to escape his clutches.

The spectre of Sammy's illness lay before her; there was no way around it without Lucio's help, but his conditions? How was she to protect herself from further pain?

She'd been gutted by their last break-up. It had taken her months to lift herself out of the abyss of depression that had almost consumed her. Could she risk her sanity to go down that path again?

'I need some time to get used to…to this,' she said. 'I have to organise Sammy's hospital admission and I—'

'I have already done that.'

'What?' She stared at him.

'In the context of the urgency I thought it best to get the ball rolling as soon as possible. His surgery will be performed early next week.'

'You had no right!'

'I had every right. Apart from yourself and Jenny, I am his next of kin in this country.'

There was no argument she could make to counteract his statement.

She realised with a sudden jolt of awareness—he was right. He was Sammy's nearest male relative and there was nothing she could do to change the fact.

'There is no point arguing to score points,' he continued. 'You are under a great deal of stress just now. I thought it would help you if I made the necessary arrangements.'

His calm deliberation made her earlier outburst seem childish and irresponsible in comparison. He made her feel as if she were somehow lacking as a parent, putting petty arguments ahead of her child's health.

'Thank you,' she mumbled grudgingly.

'I have informed the hospital that I will be responsible for all Sammy's expenses. I have also opened an account for you.' He reached into his top pocket and handed her a bank card. 'Your birth date is the pin number. There are more than sufficient funds in there to buy suitable clothes for yourself, Sammy and Jenny.'

'I don't want it.' She thrust it back at him.

He took her hand and, unpeeling her tight fingers one by one, placed the card across her palm before closing her fingers back over it. 'You will take it and use it, understood?'

She gave him a resentful scowl. 'What sort of clothes do you want me to buy? Something to titillate you?'

'You don't need clothes to do that.'

Her face burned with shame as she recalled the hateful photographs.

'I can't do this,' she said with a helpless flutter of her hands. 'I can't pretend to be your mistress like this.'

'You will not be pretending,' he assured her. 'I will make sure of that.'

She stared at him in consternation. Was that to be his final revenge, to make her want him and love him all over again?

'You can't do this to me, Lucio.' She was close to tears once more. 'You can't destroy me like this.'

'I don't want to destroy you,' he said. 'I want to possess you. I want to make you ache the way I have ached for four years. I want to purge the vision of you in Carlo's bed for ever from my mind.'

'You are going to destroy me.' Her voice was just a whisper of sound, her shoulders slumping as she accepted her fate. 'You are going to destroy me.'

Lucio stood silently before her, his dark gaze focusing on her bent head.

'Anna.'

She lifted her head and met his eyes. 'Don't make me hate you,' she pleaded.

'You already hate me so what have I got to lose?'

It was a moot point because she could never truly hate him. She loved him as she had always loved him—unreservedly, unguardedly, totally.

'I can't take much more, Lucio.' She caught her bottom lip between her teeth. 'Don't make me beg.'

His expression hardened as he reached for her, pulling her into the hard wall of his body. 'I will not be satisfied until I hear you beg.' His voice was a low growl as he bent his head to hers and captured her mouth beneath the firm intent of his.

She felt the thrust of his tongue into her mouth sending her senses into instant overdrive. She had no way to counteract his touch. She had no defences with which to hold him off. As soon as his lips met hers she was lost like tinder to a greedy flame, the fuel of need racing through her with fiery intent.

She was melting like a candle under the impact of a blowtorch, her insides pooling, her spine collapsing, pitching her forward against him, where his body throbbed with its need against hers.

His hardness, her softness, a delicious combination which she knew from experience had paradise at its culmination.

'I have longed for this,' he groaned as his hand sought the thrust of her breast. 'I have never forgotten what it is to feel you beneath me, writhing with need.'

It was a need only he could awaken. In spite of what his brother Carlo had said had happened between them, she knew she could never feel this way about anyone else. Her senses came alive with the brush of his fingers, the sweep of his tongue. Need clawed its way through her, clamouring for release, a release she knew only he could give.

His mouth came back to hers with renewed purpose, drawing from her a response she hadn't intended giving. His tongue found hers and played with it, his teeth nipping at it gently, inciting her to fight back.

She took up the challenge with a vengeance, her teeth grazing his tongue and then his full bottom lip.

'You little wildcat,' he groaned against her mouth. 'Do you want to hurt me, *cara?*'

'I would like to kill you,' she breathed against the surface of his lips.

'Kill me, then.' He smiled a lazy smile just above her mouth. 'I will die happy.'

She bit him—hard, her teeth sinking into his lip until she tasted blood.

'You want to fight dirty?' he asked, licking his savaged lip, the movement of his tongue making her desire for him unmanageable. 'You want to bite and scratch and claw at me?'

'I hate you!' she gasped as his teeth sought her nipple through her blouse, her fingers clawing for a foothold in the dark pelt of his hair. 'I hate you.'

'I love the way you hate me,' he said against her breast. 'Your body hates me so fervently I can feel it throbbing with pent-up emotion.'

She was betraying herself with every beat of her thunderous heart but there was nothing she could do to stop it.

'Sammy and Jenny will be back any minute,' she reminded him, trying desperately to push him away.

He stepped away from her with an ease she privately envied.

'I remember a time when you wouldn't have been such a spoilsport,' he chided her playfully. 'You would have scoffed at the threat of exposure and gone for it with all the passion of your nature.'

'I was stupid to fall for your charm,' she said.

'You were even more unwise to fall for my brother's.'

'According to him, I was the one who lured him into temptation.' She gave him a quelling look. 'You can't have it both ways, Lucio.'

'I have personal experience of your irresistible lures,' he returned. 'Greater men than me would go weak at the knees in the face of such delicious temptation.'

She turned away from the derision in his eyes, unwilling to see herself the way he saw her. She knew she wasn't an unprincipled person. She had always conducted herself with propriety…Until Carlo…It was like a blot on her copybook and there was nothing she could do to erase it.

'Please leave me alone,' she said. 'I can't bear to fight you when I'm feeling so…vulnerable.'

His eyes were like chips of ice as he looked down at her cowed figure. 'I will have my revenge, Anna. Make no mistake. I will have it, no matter how vulnerable you feel.'

She turned to look at him, her heart sinking when she saw the bitter determination in his face.

'You will not be happy until you've broken me, will you?'

His mouth tightened. 'I have my pride to consider. You should have factored that in when you opened your legs for my weak brother.'

She closed her eyes against the burning accusation of his.

'I will have my revenge,' he repeated. 'I will stop at nothing to get it.'

She could well believe it. The only trouble was—would she have the strength to bear it?

CHAPTER FOUR

THE next two days went by in a blur of activity.

Anna packed carefully, not wanting to take all of their belongings to Lucio's house, for she knew in the end they would all have to come back again.

This was a temporary arrangement; she had to remember that at all times.

He didn't want her.

He wanted revenge.

The car he had organised to fetch them arrived and within a few minutes pulled up in front of an imposing house of mansion-like proportions.

'Dis is a big house, Mummy,' Sammy said, trailing his teddy bear by one ragged arm. 'Does my daddy have a simming pool?'

Anna bent down to pick up her bag and gave him a weak smile. 'I don't know, darling, but we'll soon find out.'

The door opened and an older woman dressed all in black greeted them in heavily accented English.

'Miss Stockton, I am Rosa, Mr Ventressi's housekeeper.' She bent down to peer at Sammy. 'And this must be Sammy. Well, aren't you a spitting image of your daddy?'

'This is my sister, Jenny,' Anna said quickly, pushing Jenny forward.

'I am pleased to meet you.' Rosa bowed. 'Mr Ventressi left me instructions to make you very welcome. He is going to be late this evening.'

Typical, Anna thought as she shepherded Sammy inside the big house. He would want to stretch out her torture by making her wait for him to return, thus ensuring her nerves were at snapping point.

The housekeeper led them upstairs while the driver dealt with the luggage.

She showed Jenny into an airy, pretty room done in three shades of pink, soft billowing curtains at the huge windows adding to the feminine appeal.

Sammy's room was next door, painted in blue and white, a host of toys positioned about the place to fulfil any three-year-old's dream.

'Are deez mine?' he asked, his eyes widening as he took in the huge truck and a series of shining new model cars.

'Yes.' Rosa beamed. 'Your papa wanted you to feel at home.'

Anna felt her ire rising. She didn't like the thought of her son being bought with a whole lot of toys, and expensive ones at that.

'Your room is this way.' Rosa led the way down the hall. 'I'll leave you to settle in. I will have dinner ready in an hour.'

'Thank you, Rosa.' Anna did her best to give the house-keeper a genuine smile even though inside she felt at boil-ing-point.

Once Rosa had gone she turned around and inspected the master bedroom with a critical eye.

It was a huge room with a walk-in wardrobe along one wall and a luxuriously appointed *en suite* bathroom off the other.

The huge windows were draped with a black and white silky fabric with sophisticated pelmets and tassels, and the massive king-sized bed was covered in a matching fabric and was regally offset by a stately wing chair and sofa.

It was quite clearly the room of a very wealthy man who was used to having the very best of everything around him.

Anna felt like an alien in the room, her tired, faded clothes looking very out of place amongst such opulence.

She turned with a sigh and caught sight of her reflection in the cheval mirror near a small walnut writing table.

She looked exhausted. Her blue eyes were shadowed and her normally shiny mid-length blonde hair was dull and lifeless. Her skin looked unusually pale, as if she hadn't had a touch of sunlight for months, and her cheeks were distinctly hollow, as if food had been in short supply as well.

There was a sound behind her.

'Look, Anna!' Jenny's voice was excited as she bounced into the room. 'See what Lucio has bought for me!'

Anna turned and stared at the huge armful of gorgeous designer clothes cradled in her sister's arms.

'He bought them for me,' Jenny repeated. 'Rosa told me they are a gift.'

Toys for Sammy and clothes for Jenny...What did he think he was doing?

'You can't keep them.'

'What?' Jenny's face dropped.

Anna hardened her heart. 'I can't afford to pay for them.'

'But they are a gift,' Jenny said. 'You don't have to pay for gifts.'

'Don't I?' Her tone was deliberately cynical.

A green silk dress slipped from Jenny's grasp and landed on the floor at her feet.

'Is something wrong, Anna?'

'No,' she lied, hating herself. 'But we can't get used to this...' she indicated the wealth around them with a sweep of one hand '...this luxury, as it won't last.'

'What do you mean it won't last?' Jenny looked confused. 'Lucio is a very rich man. He can afford to be generous.'

'Jenny...' she began to sign to make her statement even

more clear '…I feel uncomfortable accepting such expensive gifts. If anything should go wrong…'

'What could possibly go wrong?' Jenny asked. 'Lucio is back in your life and Sammy is going to be well. What could possibly go wrong now?'

Oh, for the blissful ignorance of youth, Anna thought. Jenny was so innocent at nineteen, so full of romantic dreams of happy endings, but she didn't know the full story. She didn't know the dark secret that lay between Anna's past and the present, its looming shadow increasingly inescapable.

'Nothing.' She sighed. 'You're right. I'm just being silly.'

'You are tired,' Jenny said. 'It's been so hard for you with Sammy. I will try to help you more.'

Anna gave her a grateful smile. 'You help me so much as it is. I don't know what I would have done without you.'

'But I am on holidays now from university, so I can be even more help,' Jenny said. 'You will be free to concentrate on spending time with Lucio.'

Anna stared at her stricken reflection once her sister had left the room.

The very last thing she wanted to do was spend time with Lucio.

The very last thing.

Sammy was asleep before Anna had finished the story she'd been reading him. She tucked the sheets up close to his chin and kissed him softly on the cheek, unable to stop herself from feeling overwhelmed by maternal love, a love that had asked much more of her than most mothers ever had to pay, even in a lifetime.

Lucio's offer to help was laden with compromise for her. Everything in her wanted to reject his rescue plan, but between her resistance and pride lay Sammy's future.

She had to put him first even if it meant far greater hurt

than she had suffered before. After all, she had been the one to destroy their blissful happiness.

She was the guilty one.

She had slept with his brother; there was no escaping that fact.

Jenny had retired to her beautiful pink room and the housekeeper had long gone when Anna paced the sitting room floor waiting for Lucio to return.

She had considered crawling into the huge bed in the master bedroom but didn't fancy the idea of being asleep when he returned. She wanted to be on full alert when she saw him next, not have him slide into bed beside her and reach for her...

She heard the roar as his Maserati pulled into the driveway.

She heard the sound of the garage doors hissing closed with electronic precision.

She heard his firm tread across the gravelled driveway...he was at the door...his key in the lock...the heavy front door closed behind him...he was coming towards the thin beam of light shining underneath the sitting room door...

She leapt to her feet as he opened the door.

'You had no right to bribe them like that.'

Lucio closed the door behind him with such casualness as if she'd just commented on the weather.

'Good evening, *cara*.'

She drew in a prickly breath. 'Did you hear what I said?'

He tossed his suit jacket over the back of one of the cream sofas and reached for his tie. 'How did you all settle in?' he asked, loosening it with indolent grace.

She stared at him.

'Is there something wrong?' he added.

She let out her breath on a gasp. 'Of course there's something wrong! All of this is wrong! You've deliberately made it harder for me to…to…'

'To what, Anna? Sleep with me?'

She spun away in anger. 'I don't want to sleep with you.'

'Ah, but you have no choice now, do you, my love?'

She turned back to glare at him. 'Do you really think a roomful of toys for Sammy and a wardrobe full of clothes for my sister is all it would take for me to share your bed?'

His eyes were like dark chips of ice as he surveyed her outraged features. 'No, but I had thought you might recall the considerable expense I am going to with regard to your son's medical bills.'

She had no answer for that and she was sure he knew it.

He sat on one of the sofas and placed his feet on the coffee table opposite, his arms going behind his head in a Lord-of-all-he-surveys manner.

'Are you having last minute thoughts about our arrangement?' he asked.

'It all seems so horribly cold-blooded,' she said. 'You will be using me out of hate.'

'And why should I not hate you?' he asked.

She avoided his pointed look. 'No one is perfect. Everyone makes mistakes, it's part of being human.'

'Some mistakes incur a price,' he said. 'And you are the one I've selected to pay it.'

'What about your brother?' She turned on him. 'What price has he had to pay?'

His jaw tightened as he held her heated look. 'Carlo has paid the price of not even knowing he has a son. I cannot think of a worse punishment than that.'

She felt the breath leak out of her chest like wind out of a sail.

'So, whatever way you look at it, it's all my fault.'

'Yes.' He swung his long legs off the coffee table and stood up, his height instantly shrinking the spacious room.

'It is your fault. You were promised to me and you betrayed that promise.'

'I didn't do it alone!' She felt close to tears, frustrated at how little she remembered of that fateful night.

'Carlo is a normal red-blooded man,' he said. 'You offered him a temptation too hard to resist. He apologised to me for what he'd inadvertently done.'

'Inadvertently?' She gave him an incredulous look. 'He plied me with champagne and you call it inadvertent?'

His mouth thinned as he looked down at her. 'You didn't have to drink it.'

'And he didn't have to…to…' tears sprouted in her eyes and she brushed at them with a furious hand.

A tiny nerve pulsed at the edge of his hard mouth.

'As you said previously, what is done is done and cannot be changed. We have to move forward to what is here and now.'

'What is here and now is blackmail and bribery!'

'So?' He gave a shrug of one shoulder as if it couldn't mean less to him. 'This is what we now have and out of it shall the wrongs of the past be righted.'

'You're making it sound so positively feudal! This is the modern world, Lucio. We don't do an eye for an eye any more.'

'I will not be happy until I feel you have paid for what you did to me.'

'I have paid!' She felt like screaming the words at him. 'I have paid more than you'll ever know.'

'Not according to my account.'

She clenched her fists at her sides in frustration and anger. 'All right, then.' She glowered at him challengingly, 'Get it over with. Do what you have to do and be done with it.'

He stood immobile, his expression mask-like, his dark eyes hooded.

'What are you waiting for?' She kicked off her shoes and

reached for the buttons on her blouse. 'Isn't this what you wanted, Lucio?' She tossed her blouse to the floor and reached for the waistband of her faded jeans. 'Why don't we get it over with right here and right now so I can stop agonising over when you're finally going to pounce.' She stepped out of her jeans, standing before him in just her underwear.

Still he didn't move.

'What's wrong, Lucio?' she goaded him recklessly. 'Isn't my tired old underwear to your taste? Why don't you rip it from my body and have your wicked way with me? What's stopping you? Are you gutless, after all? Don't tell me your brother has more fire in his belly than—'

He moved so quickly she didn't have time to finish her sentence, the force of his body colliding with hers sending her backwards to the wall behind her, her gasp of surprise swallowed by the descent of his mouth. It was a kiss of hatred.

He wanted revenge and a part of her accepted her fate with resignation. She felt she needed to be punished for what she had done to his pride, but another part of her still wished things were different between them.

She wanted to feel his mouth on hers in love, not retribution. She wanted to feel his arms around her in adoration, not control and subjugation. She wanted to feel his body pressed to hers in desire, not revenge.

His tongue made its way through the barrier of her tightly compressed lips and her last resistance was gone. The seduction of her senses was her final undoing; she had no way of fighting now.

Need clamoured inside her searching for a way out. Her breasts swelled under the tight onslaught of his hands as he shaped her, the buds of her nipples like twin points of pain until his thumb found them and moved over them repeatedly, instantly soothing their ache.

She felt her bra fall from her body and the warmth of his hands on her bare flesh, the aching need between her thighs rising to unmanageable proportions as he nudged between them with a strongly muscled leg.

He reached down and tore her panties away from her, leaving them to fall around her ankles as he unleashed his maleness.

She felt the heat of his satin skin against her as he sought her liquid warmth, pushing through her tender folds with an urgency that both shocked and thrilled her.

He groaned above her mouth as he went deeper, the strong glide of his body drawing an involuntary breathless gasp from her lips.

Lucio increased his pace and she was caught up in a maelstrom of sensation, unable to stop the feelings of delight rushing through her.

He filled her completely, stretching her to accommodate his strong length. He was relentless in his pursuit of pleasure, driven in his need for completion, ruthless in his pinning of her to the wall with every deep thrust into her moist tenderness.

'It's me you want.' He accompanied the words with another deep nudge of his body within hers. 'And it's me you will have, time and time again until I have had enough of you.'

She gasped at the strength of his movements, her body not used to the urgency after years of celibacy. His body caught at her, dragging against her in a mixture of both pleasure and pain.

She flinched just the once and he stilled his movements momentarily, his eyes raking hers. 'What's wrong, Anna? Am I not measuring up to Carlo? Is that it?'

'No...'

'What is it?' He thrust again, but more gently this time. 'Are you thinking about him?'

'No…' Her fingers dug into his shoulders.

'I cannot bear that you would think of him when I am inside you,' he growled. 'I want to fill you with me so you cannot have room for anyone else.'

She wanted to tell him there had never been room for anyone else but how could she be sure it was true? She'd apparently gone quite willingly to his brother's bed, stayed the whole night and conceived a child as a result. How could she trust her feelings after that?

'I want you to scream my name.' He surged again. 'I want you to beg for me to complete you.'

She bit down hard on her lip to stop herself from crying out, her pride refusing to allow him the satisfaction of knowing his effect on her senses.

'Don't fight me,' he breathed against the soft skin of her neck. 'Let yourself go.'

'No. I hate you.'

'But you want me all the same.'

She gasped as he reached down between them to touch her intimately. Lucio smiled as he stroked the tiny pearl of her need with expert fingers.

'I…I…'

'Come for me,' he commanded gently. 'Shudder and shiver against me like you used to do.'

'I don't want to…oh…oh…oh!'

'Yes, *cara*.' He held her shaking form against him. 'You do want to.'

She did and there was nothing she could do to stop it. Great waves of feeling swept over her, leaving her totally limbless in his arms, her body like a rag doll as the last wave cast her ashore, spent with mindless pleasure.

'Now it is my turn.' He moved within her again, reawakening her senses as if he'd turned a switch. 'I have waited for this so long.'

She felt his building tension, his tightly held control slipping further and further out of his reach as with one last deep thrust he spilled himself into her silken depths with a deep shuddering groan of release.

He withdrew from her in a single movement, leaving her unguarded, ashamed and terrifyingly vulnerable.

She hitched up her panties with as much dignity as she could and searched the floor for her bra.

She heard the rasp of his zip as he repositioned his clothing, his unhurried action speaking of his ease with the situation even while she silently cringed at her own wantonness.

'I trust Rosa has shown where you will be sleeping?' he said over one shoulder as he went to pour himself a drink.

She stared at him for a speechless moment. 'Yes...'

'Good.' He turned around and toasted her with his glass. 'To our union. May there be many in the days and nights to come.'

She drew in a breath. 'You've changed, Lucio...'

His eyes glinted dangerously as he lifted the glass to his mouth once more.

She watched the up and down movement of his lean throat and sucked in another ragged breath.

'If I have changed you have only yourself to blame.' His tone was bitter as he put his glass back down.

'I'm sorry.'

He gave her a contemptuous look. 'Sorry? What exactly is it you're apologising for?'

'I didn't mean to hurt you...'

'Didn't you?'

'Of course not.' She wrung her hands in agitation. 'I don't even remember that night.'

'You don't have to remember it,' he snarled at her. 'Carlo had the foresight to document it for you.'

She swallowed the restriction in her throat before asking, 'Have you ever wondered why he did that?'

He considered her question for a moment. 'I have asked myself that from time to time but each time I get the same answer—the answer Carlo gave me. I would never have believed it of you without the evidence of those damning pictures. Your satiated smile has tortured me for four long years. No matter what I do I cannot remove the vision of you sprawled on that bed in the aftermath of slated lust.'

She closed her eyes on the image his words evoked, nausea rising in her stomach.

'Do you know how hard it is for me to even look at my brother without thinking of how you led him astray?' he asked. 'I have done all I can to repair the damage you did to our relationship but still there are scars.'

What could she say? She was guilty as charged. He was right—the pictures told the complete story even if her memory of that night failed her.

She dragged on her jeans and slipped on her blouse haphazardly. 'I don't know what to say…'

'Don't say anything,' he snapped back. 'Do you seriously think there is anything you could say that would erase the past?'

She shook her head, lowering her gaze from the venomous hatred in his.

'You are a cheap little—'

'No!'

He slashed the air with his hand. 'You are a nothing but a temptress dressed up in angel's clothing. I fell for it as did my brother, but now our relationship is on my terms and my terms only.'

'Don't call me names.'

He lapsed into Italian and she flinched as each sharply bitten word flayed her.

'Please, Lucio,' she begged him. 'I can't take this…'

'You will take everything I dish out to you,' he said between clenched teeth. 'You owe me that, now get out of my sight.'

'Lucio…Please, I—'

'Get out!' he roared at her, slamming his fist on to the sideboard with wood-splintering force.

'But I—'

He moved towards her but she stood her ground.

'I thought I told you to get out of my sight.' The words came out like little knife flicks against her tender skin.

'I know what you told me, but I refuse to be insulted by you.'

His nostrils flared as he glared down at her defiant features. 'If I want to insult you I will do so. What bigger insult could you have given me than—'

'I don't remember doing it!' she cried. 'I don't remember a thing!'

'How very convenient.'

'You don't believe me, do you?' Her expression folded in defeat. 'You don't believe me.'

He gave a rough snort of derision as he reached for something in the drawer of the small desk next to the drinks cabinet and handed it to her.

She stared at the A4 envelope in her hands with increasing dread.

'You might have conveniently forgotten what happened that night,' he said in a blood-chilling tone, 'but perhaps these will remind you.'

With nerveless fingers she opened the envelope and pulled the first photograph out…

CHAPTER FIVE

She felt the colour drain right out of her face as her eyes fell on the first picture, the bitter bile of nausea stinging her restricted throat at the sight of herself in such a compromising pose.

'Now tell me you don't remember,' he bit out.

Her head felt tight from trying to recall that night.

She stared at the photograph but it was like looking at her double, not herself. She had absolutely no recollection of ever lying there with that vacant smile on her face, the cat-with-the-litre-of-cream smile...the hands reaching for someone who was just out of reach.

She turned to the next photograph but it was more of the same. Her body was an open invitation, her hair spread out on the pillow in wanton disarray, her mouth open and still smiling, her eyes empty.

'I'm surprised you've kept these.' She handed them back to him, not bothering to look through the rest. 'It seems to border on the masochistic, if you ask me.'

'I keep them to remind myself of how foolish I was to trust you,' he said.

'How often do you look at them?' she asked.

His eyes shifted away from hers and he stuffed the envelope back into the drawer and locked it, pocketing the key.

'I look at them whenever I am tempted to let my guard down around a beautiful woman.'

'Is that why you haven't married?'

He gave her a flinty look. 'I have no desire to trap myself in a relationship of that sort.'

'You don't want children?'

He looked away again. 'Children are an encumbrance. I want no such ties in my life.'

Anna could barely believe what she was hearing. Where was the devoted family man who had said how much he looked forward to having a son or daughter of his own?

Had he changed so much?

Had she done that to him?

'As for what just happened between us—' he cut across her agonised thoughts '—I am assuming you are using some reliable sort of contraception?'

She was glad he wasn't looking in her direction for she was sure he would see the guilty flush across her cheekbones.

'Of course.' It wasn't quite a lie; she had a packet of low-dose pills she'd been using to control her monthly cycle but she hadn't taken them as regularly as she should.

There was a small silence broken only by the chink of his glass against the brandy bottle.

Anna stood next to the sofa in a stance of complete uncertainty; she was desperate to escape his disturbing presence but unwilling to cross his path to exit the room.

Lucio turned to look at her, his dark eyes unreadable as they took in her dishevelled appearance, shadowed blue eyes and swollen mouth.

He watched in mesmerised concentration as her tongue came out to salve a tiny split in her bottom lip, a small movement she tried to hide from him.

He stepped towards her, his gut clenching unexpectedly when she flinched as he lifted his hand towards her face.

'*Cara.*' His voice came out as a velvet whisper as he gently traced the tiny injury. 'Did I do that to you?'

She averted her face and his hand fell away. 'I've had worse.'

'Not from me you haven't.'

'Haven't I?' She threw him a caustic glance.

'Anna…I would never intentionally hurt you or indeed any woman.'

'Then why am I here?' she asked.

He held her look for a four second heartbeat.

'Does it hurt you to be with me, Anna?'

'You know it does…'

'Why?'

His dark gaze was too intent for her to maintain contact. She lowered her eyes and stared at the floor at his feet.

'Why does it hurt you so much to be with me?' he asked again.

She didn't trust herself to answer.

Instead she brushed past him, neatly avoiding his outflung hand as she rushed to the door, closing it behind her with exaggerated force.

Lucio stood staring at the back of the door for a full minute.

Then, in an uncharacteristic gesture of violence, he turned and threw his half-empty glass of brandy at the fireplace, shards of delicate crystal and amber fluid flying outwards to land on the cream carpet at his feet.

'*Merda!*' he swore. '*Merda!*'

Anna slept the sleep of the emotionally exhausted, waking some time after eight a.m. to find Sammy sitting on the end of the bed with one of his new toys on his lap.

'Are you awake now, Mummy?' he asked, scrambling up the bed to snuggle closer.

She smiled as she brushed her hair out of her eyes, making room for him beside her. 'Why didn't you wake me? Have you been sitting there for long?'

'Daddy told me not to wake you,' he said with an air of importance. 'He said you were stremely tired and needed to sleep.'

A funny sensation passed through her stomach at the thought of Lucio considering her needs, but she just as quickly squashed it, unwilling to allow herself to see him in anything other than a negative light.

'Well, I'm awake now,' she said and ruffled his dark hair. 'Where's Auntie Jenny?'

'She's helping Rosa with breakfast. Are you going to get up now?'

Anna secretly wished she could burrow back under the covers and not come out for a week, but in a few short days her son was facing surgery and there was so much to see to.

'I'm up.' She swung her legs over the side. 'I think.'

Sammy leaned forward and peered at her bottom lip. 'What's dat?' His little finger pointed to the tiny cut.

'I…I bit my lip.'

'Silly Mummy.' He smiled and patted her hand.

There was a sound at the door and Anna looked up to see the dark, inscrutable features of Lucio focused on her.

Sammy spun around and scampered over to him. 'I didn't wake her, Daddy, she was alweady awake.'

'Good boy.' He gave Sammy's dark curls a quick ruffle. 'Why don't you go and tell Rosa we'll be down in a few minutes, mmm?'

'OK.' He trotted off, carrying his toy truck under one arm as he went.

Anna got to her feet and reached for her threadbare dressing-gown with unsteady fingers.

'Anna.'

She tied the straps and faced him defiantly. 'Did you sleep well, Lucio?'

His eyes flickered away from hers. 'I want to apologise for my behaviour last night. I was…out of order.'

'You don't say.'

His eyes returned to her flashing, resentful ones. 'Things got out of hand...'

'*You* got out of hand,' she corrected him. 'You were intent on humiliating me. Are you happy now?'

His jaw visibly tensed as he held her fiery glare. 'I was angry last night.'

'That's no excuse and you know it.'

'I'm not making excuses.'

'I don't want to hear your apology or your excuses,' she said. 'I want to get through these next few days with Sammy without the complication of your plans for revenge colouring every moment.'

'Will you accept my assurance that I will not harm you?'

She gave him an incredulous look. 'You think I would trust you on that?'

His nostrils flared with aristocratic pride. 'You have my word.'

'Is that supposed to be some sort of guarantee? If so, it's totally inadequate. I don't trust anything that comes out of a Ventressi's mouth, least of all promises that come to nothing in the end.'

'What's that supposed to mean?' His eyes narrowed slightly.

'Go figure it out,' she threw back.

'Tell me what you mean.'

'Why should I?' she asked. 'You'll only twist it around to suit your own ends later.'

'I want to know what you meant by that statement.'

'All right—here it is.' She drew in an unsteady breath. 'Four years ago you asked me to marry you. You told me you loved me but as soon as that love was tested you bailed out. What sort of love is that? What sort of promise was that? You didn't have the guts to face what had happened; instead, you tossed me aside, never once questioning the other possibilities.'

'What other possibilities could there have been?'

She gave him an exasperated look. 'See? You still don't get it, do you? You can only see my guilty part in it—you stubbornly refuse to see me as a possible victim.'

'A victim?' His brows snapped together. 'What sort of victim writhes naked on a bed while someone takes pictures of them?'

She knew she was fast losing the argument but something in her so wanted him to search for some other explanation.

If only she could remember!

'Maybe I was...drunk.'

'Drunk?' He glared at her. 'Is that supposed to be a valid excuse for your behaviour?'

'No...of course not...but I might have inadvertently had too much to drink and—'

'I know what you're trying to do, Anna, but it won't wash with me. Painting yourself as the victim necessitates the casting of Carlo as the villain. Do you seriously think I would believe you over my brother, especially when he can recall every detail of that night while you, allegedly, cannot remember a thing?'

There was no point in continuing the argument.

It would always come back to her word over that of his brother's—she didn't have a leg to stand on.

'No, I didn't think for a moment you would believe me,' she said on the tail-end of a defeated sigh.

'Do you think I haven't done this scapegoating exercise in my own head over the last four years? Searching for an answer to a question that should never have been raised? I loved you with my whole heart. Anna, you destroyed that love. I have nothing but bitterness to offer you now. I can barely look at you without wanting to...' His words trailed off and he turned away from her, as if he didn't trust himself to even speak the words in case he was tempted to act on them.

Anna's heart squeezed painfully in her chest at the cold wall of his turned back, each and every taut line of his body communicating his distaste for her.

Shame coursed through her like a tidal wave, sweeping away her self-respect and the fragments of pride she'd clung to like a life-raft for so long.

'I am going to work.' He addressed her from the door, not even bothering to turn to face her. 'The details of Sammy's next appointment are downstairs. I will see you later.'

The door opened and closed just like her mouth but, while the door shut with an audible click, her mouth was completely silent as it closed on a choked sob of distress.

Sammy's appointment was for later that day at the hospital where the surgery was to be performed.

Anna held his tiny hand in hers as the nurse took them on a guided tour to help him understand what was going to happen next week.

'And then we put you to sleep with this machine here.' The nurse indicated the anaesthetist's equipment. 'Once you are asleep the heart surgeon will make a tiny cut in your leg, so he can put in a tiny camera that he will send to the hole in your heart, just like putting a piece back in a jigsaw puzzle.'

The nurse made it all sound so simple, and while her calm, efficient manner seemed to be allaying Sammy's fears, it was doing absolutely nothing to help Anna's. The more she heard the more she panicked. So much could go wrong! What if the anaesthetist gave him too much anaesthetic? She'd heard of people having unusual reactions, some even falling into comas. And what if he bled uncontrollably? He was so small, so vulnerable...

'Don't worry, Miss Stockton.' The nurse smiled at Anna's

stricken expression. 'We do literally thousands of this procedure every year. Sammy is in the very best of hands.'

Anna gave her a wan smile and hoped to God she was right.

When they returned to the house the escalating heat drove them out to the swimming pool in the garden. Sammy was beside himself at the sight of the pristine blue water surrounded by lush green ferns, the dappled shade at one end taking the sting out of the afternoon sun.

Anna held him close to her, not allowing him to overexert himself, content to feel his little body kicking at the water, his happy smiles doing much to calm her overstretched nerves.

Jenny was a cautious swimmer, keeping her head above water all the time as she did her version of breaststroke. Anna couldn't help smiling at her. In the last day or so she'd come right out of herself, moving from gangling teenager to blossoming womanhood. She hardly hesitated when speaking, even to Rosa, and her pretty face was nearly always smiling instead of looking pained as it had before.

Anna couldn't help thinking that perhaps the price she was paying was going to be worth it to see her son and sister finally happy. Whatever Lucio had in store for her she would face gladly if only Sammy and Jenny could be spared the sort of pain she'd had to suffer.

'Is there room in there for me?'

Anna jumped at the deep sound of Lucio's voice behind her. She turned to see his tanned, lean body, naked except for a pair of swimming trunks, which sent her imagination into overdrive. His leanly muscled body was in the peak of fitness, the sculptured muscles rippling as he brushed a lock of hair off his face.

Her breath clogged her throat as he stepped into the water,

the movement of his body disturbing the surface so that the little waves brushed across her breasts.

She felt as if he'd reached out and stroked her.

'Daddy!' Sammy squealed in delight. 'Look what I can do!' He kicked his little legs, sending water everywhere.

'Come to me, Sammy,' Lucio said, holding out his hands. 'Swim to me.'

'He can't swim,' Anna said.

'Then it's time he learned.'

'He's only three.' She met his hard look with one of her own.

Sammy gulped in a breath and threw himself towards Lucio with all tiny limbs flapping.

Lucio caught him before he went too far and, lifting him up out of the water, smiled up at him. 'Well done! I can see you are going to be a champion.'

'I love simming,' Sammy said proudly, blinking the water out of his eyes.

'Then I shall make a point of swimming every day with you,' Lucio promised.

'He won't be able to swim for a while after his surgery,' Anna pointed out.

Lucio waited until Sammy had trotted to the other end where Jenny was before he responded. 'You are too protective of him. He is a boy—he needs to explore the world.'

'He is a boy with a heart defect,' she reminded him darkly.

'I have spoken with his doctors, Anna. He is assured of a complete recovery. You are worrying too much.'

'Don't tell me not to worry about him! I'm his mother.'

'You will hold him back too much, like you've done with Jenny.'

'*What?*' She gaped at him.

'You keep her tied to you unnecessarily. She is nineteen not nine. She should be dating, going out to parties and—'

'She'd deaf, for God's sake!'

'She's deaf but not disabled, Anna.' He spoke calmly. 'She can look after herself and, in fact, needs to do so in order to take her place in the world.'

'She's vulnerable…'

'She is a strong and courageous young woman,' he said. 'She can hold her own in any company. Why not suggest she get a part-time job over the summer? It will help to bring her out of herself even more.'

'I need her to help me with Sammy,' she said. 'Childcare is so expensive. I can't work without her help on the weekends and at night.'

'You will not be working for the next three months.'

She gave him a stringent look. 'What I'm doing for you is called work in the sex industry.'

His eyes narrowed dangerously. 'Don't push your luck with me, Anna. I am a little tired of your tendency to hit out when you're feeling cornered.'

'And why wouldn't I want to hit out? You come back into my life as both judge and jury, telling me what a terrible person I am, criticising me as a mother and now as a sister. I'm so sorry for not even coming close to your exacting standards but I'm human and no way near perfect.'

'I'm not criticising you, just giving you some feedback.'

'Did I ask for your observations?' She glared at him. 'I'm doing the best I can under very trying circumstances.'

'I realise things have been difficult for you.'

'How could you possibly know what it's been like for me?' she asked. 'You come from a wealthy background; you've never had to think where the next meal is going to come from and who is going to pay for it. You're surrounded by the best life can offer and yet you dare to speculate on my shortcomings.'

'Anna, please…you are becoming hysterical.'

Angry tears sprouted in her eyes and she dashed at them

with her hand. 'You think this is hysterical? You haven't seen hysterical yet, so don't push me too far.'

'Mummy?' Sammy came towards her uncertainly. 'Are you sad?'

'No, darling, I'm just—'

'Come with me, Sammy.' Jenny took his hand. 'Daddy and Mummy need some time together.'

'But I want to know why Mummy is—'

'Come *on*, Sammy.'

Lucio waited until they were inside the house before turning back to Anna. 'Jenny is right. We do need some time together.'

'I don't want to be alone with you.'

'What are you frightened of?' he asked with a taunting little smile. 'That you might be tempted to feel something for me other than hate?'

'I could never feel anything for you but disgust at what you've done.'

'Careful, *cara*. Hasn't anyone told you it is not wise to insult one's benefactor? He might very well be tempted to pull the plug on his generosity.'

'*You bastard!*' she hissed at him. 'You arrogant, low bastard. You would do that, wouldn't you? Hold Sammy's health to ransom to achieve what you want.'

'You know the terms of the deal.' He spoke with implacable calm. 'You do your bit and I will do mine.'

'How can you be so callous?'

He met her fiery look with intransigence. 'You taught me well, *cara*. The day you slept with my brother you changed me for ever. If you don't like the man you see in front of you now, you have only yourself to blame.'

She gave an involuntary shiver, which had nothing whatsoever to do with the shifting sunlight. 'I can't bear to be in the company of someone with such ruthless disregard for another person's needs.'

'I am very aware of your needs, Anna,' he said. 'In fact, I am intimately acquainted with each and every one of them.'

She felt his lazy gaze slide over her, lingering on the thrust of her breasts in her worn bathers, the thin fabric, she couldn't help noticing now it was too late, doing a totally inadequate job of keeping her decent.

'I'm...cold.' She reached for the step but his hand came down on hers and turned her back to face him.

'It's close to thirty degrees in the shade.'

'I...'

'Don't run away from me.' He pulled her closer.

She couldn't breathe with him this close. His strongly muscled legs were brushing hers under the water, the masculine hairs tickling the smooth line of her thighs. She could see the tiny droplets of water clinging to his midnight-black eyelashes, could almost taste the warm firmness of his mouth as it came towards her slowly...

'No...' she breathed against the surface of his lips.

'You know you don't mean that.' He pressed his mouth to hers in a tantalising feathery movement that did nothing to settle the erratic thump of her heart.

. 'I do mean it,' she said, her voice barely audible as the afternoon breeze disturbed the shrubbery around them. 'I do mean it...'

'Perhaps if you keep saying it you will eventually convince yourself, but you won't convince me. You have a mouth that begs to be kissed, and a body that craves the mastery of a male mate.'

Desire kicked in with a spurt of heat deep inside her, making her body go weak from her neck to her knees. Just one kiss, she rationalised. They were in full view of the house. What harm could one little kiss do?

He saw the acquiescence in her gaze and captured her mouth once more, his tongue unfolding to take possession in one slow movement that sent a riot of sensation straight to her feminine core.

She felt him walk her backwards in the water until her back was up against the smooth tiles, his mouth gentle but no less determined as he supped from her mouth, taking her on a journey of rising urgency.

'You always taste so good.' His breath feathered across her swollen lips. 'I have never forgotten how good.'

She closed her eyes and pretended he loved her. It was easier that way than to face the painful truth. She had killed his love; this was all that was left of it—a passionate want for fulfilment to settle a four-year-old score of injured male pride.

His lips moved with purposeful determination over hers, drawing from her an answering desperate need. The rasp of his tongue called hers into play, teasing it, tasting it and dancing with it until her senses swam.

She felt his hands go to the strap of her bathers, deftly removing it so he could cup her straining breast. He bent his head and laved her tight nipple with his lazy tongue, the warmth of his mouth on her chilled flesh an exquisite sensation.

Her legs were going from beneath her; she could barely stand for the ache of her need as he pressed himself even closer, the hard outline of his masculine form leaving her in no uncertainty of his high state of arousal.

'You know, *cara*—' he spoke softly near the shell of her ear '—this was not such a good idea, mmm? I am aching to sink into you but we are in the range of the windows along this side of the house.'

I don't care! she wanted to cry, but clamped her traitorous mouth shut.

He stepped away from her and she shivered once more, this time with cold.

He vaulted effortlessly out of the pool and held out a hand to her. 'Come, we have some business to finish in private.'

It was impossible not to follow him. His eyes held a promise she could not ignore. No amount of reasoning on her part could cancel the magnetic pull of his body as he led her upstairs to the master bedroom.

Each step she took felt as if it were under his command, not hers, her body secretly preparing itself for his invasion even as her mind did its best to remind her of all that had happened between them.

But pride had no place where passion ruled. The scales were tipped against her—she had needs far greater than pride to be fulfilled.

He turned her in his arms once the door was closed behind them, his dark eyes burning with desire as he peeled her bathers from her with long, determined fingers.

'Tell me how much you want this, Anna.' He held the weight of her breasts in his warm hands. 'Tell me you want to feel me inside you.'

How could she deny it? Her body was doing all the talking for her anyway, her nipples so tight they almost hurt, her thighs like jelly, and her feminine folds so slick with moisture she was sure she was going to melt into a pool at his feet.

'I want…' She hesitated. 'I want…'

'Say it,' he said. 'I won't go any further until you do.'

She wanted to call his bluff but was too far gone to do so.

'I want you,' she said. 'I want you.'

He lifted her and placed her on the bed, coming down over her with his weight. 'Then, *cara*, you shall have me.'

She clawed at him with greedy fingers, tearing off his swimming trunks to get at his hard, smooth flesh. Her hands shaped him, caressing him until he sucked in a ragged breath with her increasingly bold movements.

'So my little temptress has not forgotten all I taught her,' he growled as he searched for her warmth with devastating accuracy.

She gasped as he slid into her with one deep surge of his powerful body, the full weight of him a delicious burden pressing her down…down…

'You are so ready for me,' he groaned against her mouth, 'so moist and warm.'

'You don't play fair, Lucio.' She whimpered as he sought the delicate pulse between her thighs.

'Do I not?' He smiled above her mouth. 'But you will forgive me in the end. You want this too much.'

She did want it. She wanted it all. She wanted him to pleasure her the way he used to do, but she wanted more. She wanted him to forgive her, to love her in spite of her one mistake…a mistake of which she still had no memory.

'Please…' She was teetering on the edge, all her muscles straining to get to the highest pinnacle…closer and closer…

He pushed her over with a deep thrust of his body, her senses instantly singing with the rapturous chorus of release.

Lucio waited for as long as he dared before he followed her to paradise, his body tensing against hers in shuddering pleasure as each ecstatic expulsion was executed.

He rolled away and flung a hand across his eyes, his chest moving up and down with his laboured breathing.

Anna edged away, suddenly embarrassed at how she'd responded to him, clawing at him, almost begging like some sort of cheap little tart who had no principles.

'Where are you going?' Lucio caught her before she leapt off the bed.

She gave his fingers around her wrist an arctic glare. 'I need to use the bathroom.' She raised her eyes to his as she tugged on his hold, 'Is that all right with you?'

He let her hand drop and lay back on the pillows, his eyes following her as she stalked stiff-backed to the *en suite* bathroom. 'I would advise against sulking, Anna,' he called after her. 'Don't forget, you are the one with the most at stake.'

She turned around to glare at him. 'Twist the knife all you like. I'm not afraid of you.'

He smiled a hateful smile and folded his arms behind his head in a pose of such masculine superiority she wanted to hit him with something. 'Be afraid, Anna,' he drawled, his eyes twinkling at her goadingly. 'Be very afraid.'

She slammed the bathroom door on him but even when she had the shower running on full she was sure she could still hear the sound of his mocking laughter.

CHAPTER SIX

ANNA barely slept the night before the morning of Sammy's operation, tossing and fighting with the bedclothes until she tumbled out of bed with darkened eyes and sallow skin.

In spite of their physical intimacy, Lucio hadn't slept with her for a full night, preferring to leave the big bed to sleep elsewhere. Anna fought against acknowledging her disappointment even to herself, much less to him. She simply rolled over each time and pretended to be asleep although, invariably, it was a long time before she managed to relax enough to do so.

Sammy wasn't allowed any breakfast so, after taking a couple of sips of a cup of tea she had no stomach for, Lucio led the way out to his car.

'Stop worrying, Anna,' he chided her gently as he held the door for her. 'Sammy is going to come out of this like the little champion he is.'

'I can't help it.' She bit her lip. 'He's so little…it's such a big operation.'

'It's relatively simple compared to what it was a few years ago,' he reminded her. 'Back then it was open chest surgery and weeks, if not months, of rehabilitation. Sammy will be in and out of there before you know it.'

She wished she could have his confidence.

Sammy chatted excitedly all the way to the hospital, his sense of importance increasing by the minute by all the attention he was receiving.

'Will you be there when I wake up, Mummy?' he piped up from his child seat in the back.

'Of course I will, darling.'

'I will be there too, Sammy,' Lucio reassured him.

Anna slanted him a glance and muttered in an undertone, 'Don't make promises you have no intention of keeping.'

He returned her look. 'You think I don't care about him, don't you?'

'He's not your child, Lucio. Caring about him won't make him yours.'

His fingers on the steering wheel tightened. 'Do you think I don't know that?'

She turned away from his grim expression, her hands tightening in her lap.

'You throw that in my face once more, Anna, and I will not be answerable to the consequences.' His voice was a savage undertone.

There was a strained little voice from the back. 'Are you and Daddy fighting?'

Anna threw Lucio a see-what-you've-done-now look and clamped her lips together.

'No, poppet,' Lucio said with a little smile. 'Mummy and Daddy really do love each other. We just have a little trouble communicating it.'

'What's commun…comm…that word mean?' Sammy asked.

'It means understanding where the other person is coming from,' Lucio explained. 'It can take years to get it right.'

Anna tossed her head and stared sightlessly at the view outside.

Mummy and Daddy love each other, indeed.

'…and now he's asleep,' the anaesthetist said as he adjusted the mask over Sammy's little face. 'Why don't you and your husband have a coffee in the parents' room and we'll come and see you when we have your little man sorted out.'

Anna wanted to say, he's not my husband and nor is

Sammy his little man, but the words died in the back of her throat.

'Come on, darling.' Lucio took her arm and led her from the operating suite.

Once outside, they stripped off the theatre gear they'd been requested to wear as they accompanied Sammy to theatre.

'He'll be fine, Anna.'

She took off her overshoes and tossed them in the bin provided. 'I can't help thinking that somehow this is all my fault.'

'What do you mean?'

She scrunched up her cap and sent it too in the direction of the bin. 'I'm being punished for…for…'

'That's ridiculous.'

'Is it?' she asked.

'Of course it is.'

'But you're punishing me,' she said, looking at him. 'Making me pay for my sins, you said.'

He looked uncomfortable under her challenging scrutiny. 'I was angry. People say all sorts of things when they're angry.'

She sat on the only chair and put her head into her hands. 'I just wish I could turn back the clock…'

She felt his hand touch the back of her head. 'We can't, no matter how much we'd like to.'

'If he dies I will never forgive myself.'

'He won't die.'

'I won't forgive myself either way.'

'Stop this, Anna.'

'How can I stop it?' She lifted her head to look at him, her eyes shadowed with regret. 'I can't move forward because I don't remember what happened.'

'I don't wish to have this discussion now,' he said. 'It's pointless.'

'But don't you see how it keeps coming back to this?' she asked.

'There will be a time when this ceases to be important.'

Yes, she thought dejectedly—when you've gone back to Italy to pick up the reins of your own life, leaving me to heartache and a lifetime of loneliness. She chewed the jagged edge of one nail.

'Don't.' He pulled her hand away from her mouth, lifting it to inspect it, his long fingers warm against the chill of hers. 'You used to have such lovely nails.'

'Yes, well, I used to be such a lovely girl back then too, or so you said.'

He frowned at the bitterness in her tone and dropped her hand. 'We seal our fate with the choices we make, Anna. There's no escaping that fact.'

She bit her lip on her stinging reply. What was the point of arguing with him? She had done the wrong thing, not him. She had betrayed him and had been paying for it ever since.

'Everything went very well.' The cardiac surgeon took off his theatre cap and smiled at them both. 'You can see him in Recovery now, but he'll be sleepy for quite a while yet.'

Anna leapt to her feet. 'He's going to be all right?'

'Of course he is,' the doctor reassured her. 'Mind you, I'm glad you brought his surgery forward the way you did. It doesn't do to wait around in these sorts of cases.'

Anna stood gazing down at her sleeping son, the various tubes and tapes on his little body tearing at her heartstrings. She owed Lucio so much. He had saved Sammy's life as surely as the surgeon who'd performed the operation. How would she ever be able to thank him?

Lucio left her with Sammy to speak with the nursing staff, coming back a few minutes later with a container of juice for her. 'I thought you might be thirsty.'

She took the juice with a grateful look. 'You must have been reading my mind.'

'How is he?' He took the other chair and leant his arms on his knees.

'Still sleeping.' She unscrewed the top of the juice and took a sip. 'He made a murmur once or twice but the nurse said they doped him up to keep him still. He won't wake for hours.'

'Maybe we should leave and come back in the morning,' he suggested.

She swung around to face him. 'I can't leave him!'

'Anna…you're exhausted. You won't be doing him any good by fainting with exhaustion.'

'I don't want to leave him.'

He got to his feet and made his way back to the door. 'Have it your way, then, but I think you're going to regret it.'

'There are other things I regret much more,' she shot back as he opened the door.

He turned back to look at her for an endless moment. 'I know exactly what you mean,' he said, and stepping through closed the door behind him.

It was a long night.

Sammy slept through in blissful ignorance of his mother's lonely vigil by his bedside, a vigil broken occasionally by the visit of one of the nursing staff to check on his condition.

'You look tired,' a nurse on the graveyard shift observed. 'Would you like me to find somewhere for you lie down?'

Anna shook her head. 'I want to be here in case he wakes up.'

The nurse put Sammy's chart back on the wall above his head. 'I don't think there's much likelihood of this young man waking up too soon. Dr Frentalle likes to keep infants quiet until the femoral artery puncture site settles down.

Movement can set off a major bleed so it's best to be conservative in management of the first few hours.'

'I'd like to stay here all the same,' Anna said, turning back to Sammy's sleeping form. 'It gives me time to think.'

'I could do with some of that myself.' The nurse gave a wry smile. 'Call us if you need anything.'

Anna gave her an answering smile and, once the nurse had left, sat and watched Sammy until her eyes started to close and her thoughts drifted back to a night four years ago...

'...Come on, Anna.' Carlo's voice was cajoling, 'Surely you're not going to refuse a drink with your future brother-in-law?'

'I really don't think—'

'What are you afraid of?' He smiled a wolf's smile as he handed her a glass of chilled champagne. 'I won't eat you.'

'I didn't think anything of the—'

'You don't like me, though, do you, sweet Anna?' he asked, watching her like a hawk does his next meal.

'You're Lucio's brother,' Anna said, lowering her nervous gaze from the hard glitter of his. 'You're family...'

'Family, eh?' Slightly crooked teeth appeared between full lips stretched into a fabricated smile. 'I must say, I don't think of you along the same lines as my sister Giulia.' His eyes ran over her suggestively. 'Not the same lines at all.'

She began to rise. 'I must go and find Jenny—'

His hand snaked out and took her arm. 'What's the hurry? Don't you want to stay and talk to your new big brother?'

'I—' His hold was impossible to throw off and she began to feel distinctly uncomfortable.

'Your sister is a pretty little thing, isn't she?' he asked as one of his thick fingers stroked along the fluttering pulse in her wrist.

Anna didn't care for the predatory tone in his voice. She'd

seen his narrow-eyed gaze on her sister when he thought no one was looking. Jenny was only fifteen and her protected upbringing and her hearing problems left her totally vulnerable to the sort of wiles of someone like Carlo. Anna determined right then and there she would make sure he didn't get a chance to act on his intimations, even if she had to suffer his company herself.

'I think I will have that champagne after all.' She gave him what she hoped was an encouraging smile.

His eyes glinted as he handed the glass of bubbling liquid. 'I knew you wouldn't say no. Lucio would want me to entertain you in his absence—it's a matter of family honour, you understand. I am the family head when Lucio is out of the country. What do you call it in Australia? The boss?'

'Something like that.' She gritted her teeth at his patriarchal arrogance and lifted the champagne to her lips.

'You are a very lucky young woman, Anna,' he said after she'd taken a couple more sips. 'You are marrying into one of Italy's aristocratic dynasties. The Ventressis are known all over the world for their business acumen. You will want for nothing as Lucio's wife.'

'I'm not marrying him for his money,' she felt compelled to say.

One of his dark brows rose in what could only be described as world-weary cynicism. 'You are going to find it hard to convince most people of that. All women want security. Throughout history women just like you have chosen husbands for that reason alone. It is part of evolution is it not? The survival of the richest?'

'The fittest,' she corrected him. 'Survival of the fittest.'

'Ah, yes,' he mused. 'One must indeed be very fit to entertain a young and passionate wife.'

Anna took another deep sip of her champagne to disguise her increasing discomfiture with the way the conversation was turning.

'I've heard you, you know,' he said.

Her fingers around the stem of her glass tightened. 'W...what?'

His eyes flicked to her breasts and back to her widened eyes. 'It is fortunate your sister is deaf for she might be a little shocked at her big sister's hearty response to her fiancé's attentions, would she not?'

Anna was too embarrassed to think of a suitable response. *He'd heard her and Lucio making love?*

'But I am not shocked.' He smiled. 'I am delighted for my brother. I am jealous, but then maybe little Jenny will be just like her sister, no?'

'*No!*' Anna put the glass down with a snap.

'What is wrong? You don't think I would be a good lover?'

'No, I mean yes...I—'

'Come now, Anna, don't be so hard on your new brother. Do you not find me attractive? People always say how Lucio and I are alike. Are you not the least bit interested in whether we are alike in...what shall I say? Other more intimate ways?'

Her head felt strange all of a sudden and her limbs weak. 'I don't think this is a good—' She clutched at the edge of the sofa to stop herself tilting towards him.

'What is wrong, little one?' His voice was all concern.

'Nothing.' She took a couple of calming breaths. 'I felt faint, that's all.'

'It is all this talk of love that is disturbing you. You are missing your lover, no?'

She blinked away her blurred vision and concentrated on his swimming features. 'Yes...yes, I miss him.'

'Don't worry, *cara a mio*. I will take very great care of you while he is away. Do you need to lie down?'

'No...'

'What about another drink?'

She shook her head but another glass of champagne was pressed into her hands and she took it, not wanting to offend him.

'You are on edge, Anna,' he said as she sipped the drink. 'You need to relax. You are amongst family; you have nothing to fear.'

She was starting to relax, her shoulders and neck loosening as she took another sip of the delicious champagne.

'Do you…have a girlfriend, Carlo?' she asked, filling the silence.

His eyes met hers across the short distance that separated them. 'I have many girlfriends. I am what you say…a playtoy?'

She giggled at his mistake. 'A playboy, Carlo. What you are is a playboy.'

'Do you think so?' He grinned at her.

'Very definitely a playboy.' She twirled her glass in one hand as she surveyed his handsome features. 'Of the very worst sort.'

He gave her a crestfallen glance. 'Now I truly am offended.'

She laughed again. 'I think it would be nearly impossible to offend someone like you. You are too streetwise.'

'Streetwise? What does that mean?'

She finished her champagne before she answered. 'It means you are very familiar with the ways of the world.'

'Ah, but is that not a good thing?'

She gave a casual shrug of one slim shoulder as he reached to refill her glass. 'I guess one can never be too rich, Carlo, but one can very definitely be too cynical.'

'You think I am a cynic?'

'Of course you are! You think I'm marrying your brother for all the wrong reasons. That's very cynical of you.'

'Maybe you are right.' He examined the contents of his

glass. 'I have allowed some bad experiences with women to colour my judgement.'

'Have you ever been in love, Carlo?'

He raised his eyes to hers. 'It is somewhat of a legend, Anna, that the Ventressi males fall in love once in a lifetime. They love deeply and completely but if crossed in love they never forgive.'

'You didn't answer my question.'

'It is a hard question to answer.'

'You don't want to tell me?'

He smiled at her. 'I have not yet been in love, but I am on the...'

'Lookout?' she offered.

'You are very good for my English, Anna. I am learning so much from you.'

'You're a good pupil, Carlo.' She smiled and raised her glass. 'To my new brother-in-law—the erstwhile playboy of the Ventressi males.'

He raised his glass and chinked it against hers. 'To family love, Anna.'

They made their way through another bottle of French champagne, and even though Anna knew she was getting increasingly tipsy she began to relax enough to really enjoy the easy repartee of Lucio's younger brother.

Once he let his arrogant guard down she caught a glimpse of a rather nice but slightly insecure young man, a man who had constantly lived in the shadow of a high-achieving, older, more successful brother.

'Of course our lives changed for ever when our father died,' Carlo confessed, staring into his glass, his brow creased in a frown.

'It must have been very hard for you,' she said softly. 'How old were you?'

'I was Jenny's age, Giulia seventeen and Lucio nineteen.

It was such a shock, for my mother particularly, but for us all really.'

'An accident?'

He nodded. 'He was working hard to build up the business. He was on his way home from Naples and he fell asleep at the wheel. He died instantly.'

'I'm so sorry.'

He gave her a brief smile. 'You too have had your grief to bear. Lucio told me your mother has not long departed this world.'

She couldn't help smiling at the old fashioned term. Yes, her mother had departed this world—her world, the world of her two young daughters.

'Yes...I miss her terribly.'

'But you have Jenny.'

She gave him a brief smile. 'Yes...I have Jenny.'

'And now you have a new family.' He topped up her glass once more. 'You are shortly to be a Ventressi, part of one of Italy's most noble families.'

'I only hope I live up to everyone's expectations,' she said, reaching for her glass.

'Oh, I think you will,' he said and raised his glass in a toast. 'I think you will very definitely live up to everyone's expectations.'

Anna could recall very little more of that night. She remembered joining him in another toast, laughing again at one of his misuses of English, even remembered playfully correcting him and his mock-injured response.

She woke the next morning to find herself in Carlo's bed, the light from the windows too bright for her eyes, but it was nothing to the glare in Lucio's when he thrust open the door and stared down at her in disbelief.

'Anna?'

'Lucio!' She began to sit upright but suddenly realised she was totally naked.

His eyes raked her mercilessly. 'What are you doing in Carlo's bed?'

She looked at him blankly for a moment as she tried to think how she came to be in his brother's room.

'I...'

He threw a savage word in Italian at her which she loosely translated as 'slut'.

'Lucio, I—'

His jaw was tight with barely controlled rage, 'You shameless little gold-digger. Carlo was right about you. You are nothing but trash—on the hunt for a rich husband.'

'No!' She clutched at the sheet to cover her shame.

He gave her a disparaging glance that cut her to the quick. 'I turn my back and you seduce my brother in my absence!'

'No!' She scrambled from the bed, snatching up the sheet to cover herself haphazardly. 'Lucio, I didn't do—'

He cut her off with a slash of his hand. 'Do not try and dig yourself out of this hole. Carlo has told me it all.'

'Told you what?' She gripped the sheet with shaking fingers.

His eyes raked her from head to foot. 'He told me how you came on to him.'

'I didn't!'

His nostrils flared with distaste. 'He was inconsolable about what you'd led him to do.'

She opened and closed her mouth.

'He is so deeply ashamed that he was caught off guard.'

She couldn't get her head around it. *Carlo had said she'd...*

'And you believed him?' She gaped at him.

'Why would I not believe him?' he asked. 'He is my brother.'

Why, indeed? she thought, but didn't articulate it.

'I don't remember what happened last night, Lucio, but I know I did not sleep with your brother.'

'Do not lie to me!' he roared at her. 'You gave yourself to him in his moment of weakness. He is traumatised by what occurred.'

Carlo? Traumatised?

'I can explain…'

'Do you think I want to hear your explanations?'

'I—'

'You disgust me.'

'Lucio, I didn't—'

'I don't want to continue this discussion,' he interjected. 'I have organised for you and your sister to leave immediately.'

'But—'

'Do you think I could overlook such an indiscretion?'

'I didn't do any—'

'Damn you to hell!' he shouted. 'I loved you, Anna. How could you do this to me?'

'Lucio…' She reached out a hand to him pleadingly.

He brushed it aside with a furious gesture. 'I never want to see you again. Do you hear me? I never want to see your treacherous face again. You will leave in the morning; the servants are, as we speak, packing your bags. I never want to hear your name mentioned in my presence again.'

'But Lucio, I—'

'Get out of my sight, Anna,' he warned. 'For I am this close—' he held up two fingers in a pinch '—to losing all control with you.'

She stared at him in consternation. He was like a stranger to her. Gone was the gentle lover of a few days ago; in his place was a man stretched to the limits of control, his pulsing anger like a force separating them.

'I didn't sleep with—'

'Get out before I throw you out.'

'I love you, Lucio!'

His dark gaze stripped her of all dignity. 'You are worth-

less. Take your sister and get out of my house before I call
the authorities. You have brought shame on the Ventressi
name and I will not forgive you for it.'

He turned away from her and strode towards the door of
his brother's bedroom, his back rigid with injured pride.

'I didn't sleep with Carlo…' Her words trailed away in-
effectually. 'I didn't…'

But he had gone.

Anna woke to find Lucio beside Sammy's bed, one of his
long-fingered hands holding the tiny starfish hand of her
infant son.

'He is doing very well, the nursing staff tell me,' he said.

She blinked the drowsiness out of her eyes and looked
up at him. 'How long have you been here?'

He gave her an unreadable look. 'Long enough to hear
you murmur my brother's name in your sleep.'

She lowered her eyes to stare at the floor, not sure how
to respond.

'No doubt you are feeling guilty for not telling him about
the existence of his son,' he observed.

She bit her lip in agitation. It had crossed her mind many
times to inform Carlo of Sammy's existence. However, her
firsthand experience of the cold-blooded ruthlessness of the
Ventressis had always prevented her from acting on the impulse. The Ventressi wealth and influence meant they would
have had no trouble taking charge if she'd told them of her
son's birth, and even now it was apparent to her she still
stood on increasingly unsteady ground.

She was a single mother with few resources; it wasn't too
hard to imagine an Italian legal advisor insisting Sammy
had a right to his paternal origins, even though the circumstances of his conception were hardly what one could describe as ideal. The very fact that she'd fallen pregnant to
one brother whilst engaged to the other would have worked

against her suitability as a mother, leaving her at the mercy of a judge's decision in a plea for custody.

'I'm surprised you haven't told him yourself,' she said after a tight silence.

He gave her a hard look from beneath dark lashes. 'I told you before—Carlo is happily married with a child expected in a matter of weeks. I do not think he needs to have his marriage compromised at this time by such a disclosure.'

'Have you told him you're…living with me?' she asked.

'I have told him what he needs to know.'

'Which is?'

'I told him we are having an affair.'

Anna could feel the heat rising in her cheeks at his blunt statement. 'What did he say to that?'

'He was surprised…Even a little shocked, maybe.'

'I can just imagine.' Her tone was deliberately dry. 'What did he say? What a fool you are to get your fingers burnt all over again?'

He watched her for a long moment before answering. 'No, he didn't say anything of that nature.'

Anna became increasingly aware of the stretching silence, its long drawn out passage measured by the steady beeps of Sammy's ECG monitor beside them.

'My brother finds it very painful to speak of that night,' he said at last. 'It seems he feels the burden of guilt much more keenly than you.'

Her head came up at that. 'What do you know of what I might be feeling? What can you possibly know? You're a man—no doubt you've slept with hundreds of women, never once stopping to consider the implications. I made one mistake! A mistake I can't even recall making, even though there is more than enough evidence to convict me. But because I'm a woman I'm judged more harshly. I have a child, a child who was conceived out of wedlock, a child who doesn't have a normal relationship with his father because of one stupid slip-up. Don't tell me your brother feels more guilt than me. I feel enough guilt for both of us.'

'Carlo must not find out about Sammy,' he said. 'His wife would not understand. It would cause untold trouble in the family.'

'Did I ever say I wanted him to know?' she asked. 'I have not asked for anything from the Ventressis. I'd rather scrub my fingers to the knuckles than take a handout from any of you.'

'I will adopt Sammy as my own child.'

Anna swivelled her head to stare at him. '*What?*'

He drew in a deep breath and met her steely gaze. 'I will marry you and take on Sammy as my own.'

She sprang to her feet in consternation. 'You would go that far to protect your brother from the truth?'

'I will do anything to protect my family from exploitation. We shall marry as soon as Sammy is out of hospital. I will claim him as my own. No one will question it.'

'No one but me, that is!' she pointed out. 'I can't marry you!'

'Why ever not?'

She gaped at him incredulously. 'You can *ask* that?'

He gave a dismissive shrug. 'You will soon get used to the idea.'

'I will never get used to it!' she said. 'I can't think of anything worse.'

'Can't you?' His dark eyes hardened. 'Think about it, Anna. I could engage the best legal team to whip Sammy away from you within days of applying for custody. You're reputation will be examined and the truth will come out. You seduced my brother and have kept the existence of his son a secret from him. You are living on the breadline, your sister is—'

'Don't you dare to drag Jenny into this!' she railed. 'She has nothing whatsoever to do with this.'

He gave her an arrogant look down the length of his nose. 'I will use any means at my disposal to make sure you are held to account for what you've done.'

She swallowed the lump of fear in her throat. 'You'd go that far to achieve your ends? Even to the point of marrying me?'

He gave her a smile that chilled her to the marrow.

'I will do whatever it takes to have you back in my bed—permanently. Make no mistake, Anna. I will extract my revenge piece by piece until you are in no doubt of which side your bread is buttered. I will own you, control you and make love to you whenever and however I feel like it. You will be mine, body and soul.'

'You can't do this!'

'Watch me.'

'This is outrageous!'

'This is justice.'

'I can't believe how you've changed,' she said with a desperate edge to her tone. 'You used to be so...so...'

'I used to be a fool,' he said. 'But I am wiser now. I know exactly how to deal with someone like you now. You are mine now, Anna. Don't ever forget that. You are mine.'

CHAPTER SEVEN

THE next week was a form of torture for Anna. Each day spent by Sammy's bedside was hard enough to deal with without the added burden of Lucio's plans hanging over her head like the sword of Damocles.

She couldn't escape her anguish over his plan to bring her to justice. He was after control. Control of her, control of her son, control of her responses to him as if she had no mind of her own.

She was so inextricably caught in the mesh of his net she couldn't think of a possible way out of it. Every way she turned she confronted his determined purpose. He was calling all the shots and there was nothing she could do to stop him.

She knew he could scoop Sammy away from her at a moment's notice. He would use Jenny as leverage, citing her disability, exploiting her vulnerability to achieve his own goal in securing Sammy as a Ventressi.

He would let nothing stand in his way. He wanted her to pay for her indiscretion—an indiscretion that had wounded his pride. It was his idea of justice and she would have no choice but to do as he commanded.

But marriage?

How could she go through with it? She would be committing herself to a lifetime of his disdain; every time he looked at her she would be reminded of what he thought of her, of how she'd betrayed him.

And Sammy?

Yes, he would finally have a father figure, but at what price? The secret of Sammy's paternity would lie between them like something unpleasant beneath the carpet of their lives. They would have to skirt around it, never bringing it to the surface for Sammy's sake, but it would never go away, no matter how much they tried to ignore it. She'd had a child via his brother, and he had made it very clear he could never forgive her for that.

Lucio came regularly to the hospital and Anna thought anyone watching from the outside would imagine him to be a doting father and an attentive partner to her. He brought her drinks and snacks and sat and read or played with Sammy so she could take a much needed break. In the presence of the staff he was polite and solicitous towards her, giving the impression he cared for her deeply. If only they knew of the way he'd coerced her back into his life! How, within days of Sammy leaving hospital, he planned to put a ring on her finger and a noose around her neck, thus tying her to him indefinitely.

The day before Sammy was being released she came back from a bathroom visit to find Jenny sitting beside his sleeping form with a pleased expression on her face.

'Hi, Jen.' Anna kissed her affectionately. 'You look happy; what's going on?'

'I've got a job!' Jenny signed excitedly.

Anna frowned. 'What sort of job?'

'Lucio has organised some work for me in his company. I start tomorrow.'

Anna sat on the edge of Sammy's bed and faced her. 'Are you sure that's wise?'

'What's the matter?' Jenny looked confused. 'I thought you would be pleased. After all, you and Lucio are getting married now, so it's all worked out. I can work for the summer before I go back to university. It will be good experience for me.'

'He told you we were getting married?'

'Yes,' Jenny said. 'He said he had a special licence to get married next week.'

'Next week!' she gasped.

Jenny gave her a funny look. 'Are you not happy, Anna? You love him, don't you? You've never stopped loving him so why are you balking at it now?'

She gnawed her lip, seriously considering telling her sister the full and gory details of what had happened, but before she could frame her response Jenny continued signing. 'I realise he is still angry over you not telling him about Sammy but he is prepared to put that aside to give your relationship another chance. Surely you owe him that, especially as he's paying for Sammy's surgery?'

What could she say? Yes, she did owe him. She owed him more than she could ever repay but that still didn't change what lay between them—the bitterness, the pain…the betrayal.

'You're right, of course,' she said instead. 'I'm worrying about nothing. It will all work out in the end—it has to.'

'You are so exhausted.' Jenny touched her hand. 'Why don't you go home and have a decent sleep? I can stay with Sammy until the morning.'

Anna squeezed her sister's hand. 'You're such an angel, Jenny, but I really need to be here. I'm his mother, after all.'

'He has a father now,' Jenny said. 'You don't have to do this alone any more. Lucio told me he is coming in after work; he should be here shortly.'

As if she'd summoned him by mentioning his name he appeared in the doorway, his tall, imposing figure casting a shadow into the room.

'Hello, Anna.' His dark eyes sought hers. 'How is my boy?'

His boy! If only Sammy was his son, how much easier it would all be!

She stretched her mouth into the vestige of a smile. 'Dr Frentalle says he can go home tomorrow.'

'But that is wonderful.' He returned her smile.

'Why don't you take Anna out for a meal?' Jenny addressed Lucio. 'I can sit with Sammy for a couple of hours.'

'I don't think—' Anna began.

'Thank you, Jenny.' Lucio smiled. 'We won't be long, an hour and a half at the most.'

'But I—' Anna tried again.

'Let's go before Sammy wakes up.' He took her arm in an unmistakably firm hold.

Anna waited until they were well past the nurses' station before venting her spleen. She tugged herself out of his hold and threw an arctic look his way. 'I do not want to have dinner with you.'

'You need to eat,' he replied with implacable calm. 'So you might as well do so with me. After all, we'll be sharing a breakfast and dinner table for the next few years. You might as well get used to it straight away.'

'I will never get used to it. I don't even want to marry you.'

'You were quite keen on the idea four years ago.'

'You're not the same man, Lucio.'

'True, but then you are not the woman I thought I was marrying either. At least this time around I know what I'm getting.'

'You're getting nothing because I don't want to marry you.'

'You will marry me, Anna, or live with the consequences.'

'Are you threatening me?' She glared up at him.

He met her fiery look with equanimity. 'No, just reminding you of a few pertinent facts.'

'The first being you're the one in control?'

'That is, of course, a given. Do you think I would allow

you to ride roughshod over me again? I am not so foolish. I will have you on my terms for as long as I want and there is nothing you can do to stop me.'

'Isn't this taking revenge a little too far? Marrying a woman you hate?'

'Do you know something, Anna?' He gave her a penetrating look. 'I would rather marry you in hatred than live without you in love.'

She stared at him for endless moments as her brain tried to make sense of his words.

'I don't care what you feel for me; it's quite immaterial to me. I want you, simple as that,' he continued. 'You will be my wife and Sammy, for all intents and purposes, will be known as my son. I will treat him no differently from any other children we have.'

'Children?' Her mouth dropped open. 'You want to have children?'

'But of course.'

'But I—'

'Not at first,' he said, interrupting her. 'It's understandable you'd want some time to adjust.'

'I'd need a lifetime!'

'Sammy's needs are paramount just now. We can wait a while before we bring another child into the equation.'

'How very considerate of you.' Her tone dripped with sarcasm.

'What is it you are finding so distasteful, Anna? You had a child with my brother so having one or two with me shouldn't be all that difficult.'

'You're so clinical about this!' she said.

'I don't want to cloud the issue of our relationship with a pretence of feeling that just isn't there any more.'

Her heart sank at his words. His feelings weren't there any more, simple as that. He felt nothing for her now— nothing but hatred.

'We will marry next week and when Sammy has permission to fly we shall go to Rome. My family will want to welcome you formally.'

'I don't want to go to Rome.'

He didn't speak as he led the way out to his car but Anna could tell he was angry with her by the way his mouth had tightened into a thin white line. He unlocked the car and held her door for her but his eyes avoided hers as if he couldn't bear to even look at her.

'I don't want to go to Rome,' she repeated once he was in the car as well.

'I heard you the first time.' His tone was clipped as he backed out of the space.

'My home is in Australia,' she insisted. 'Jenny has uni and—'

'I did not ask you to emigrate.' He thrust the car into gear with barely controlled savagery. 'I simply told you we would be making a visit to Rome.'

'But your home is in Italy,' she said, suddenly confused. 'You said you were only going to be here for three months, so I assumed you meant—'

'I will be travelling back and forth to Italy for the next year or so,' he informed her. 'When it is convenient, you and Sammy, and even Jenny if her vacations allow, will accompany me.'

'So I'm to be a part-time wife?' She chanced a glance in his direction.

His eyes met hers briefly before he turned back to the traffic. 'Surely you didn't expect to be appointed full-time, did you?'

She had no answer to that. What had she been expecting? A promise of long-term commitment and happy ever after? She bit her lip and shifted her gaze, not trusting herself to look his way without betraying how fragile her emotions were.

'What do you fancy to eat?' he asked into the heavy silence.

'I'm not hungry.'

She heard his indrawn breath and the sound of his fingers drumming on the steering wheel.

'You don't give an inch, do you?' he asked. 'You persist in fighting me at every turn.'

'Why wouldn't I fight you?' She glared back at him. 'You're treating me like a piece on the chess board, shifting me where you like with no thought to what I might like.'

'All right.' His jaw tightened. 'What do you want?'

'I...' What did she want? How could she tell him?

'Tell me what would make you happy,' he said.

'Happy?' She tilted her head in a gesture of thinking. 'Oh yes, I remember now—happy...that emotion one feels once in a lifetime if one is extremely lucky.'

'Sarcasm is not your strong point.'

'Well, charm is definitely not one of yours.'

'I'm trying to do my level best to sort out the mess of our lives,' he ground out. 'I didn't have to help you with Sammy, you know. He is really nothing to do with me—nothing.'

'What do you want?' Her voice rose shrilly. 'Do you want a medal for what you did? So, you paid for a little kid's health care. So what? What else do you want me to do? Isn't it enough that I've slept with you and agreed to live with you for three months? What else do you want?'

His eyes met the dark fury in hers. 'What I want was destroyed four years ago.'

She blinked back the sting of bitter tears. 'I wish for once you wouldn't keep mentioning the past.'

'Why? Does it make you feel guilty? Is that why you hate me reminding you?'

She turned away with a choked sob. 'I just hate it, that's all. I just hate it.'

'Yes, well, I hate it too, but it won't go away. It's there between us, Anna, and unless we face it we will continue to trip over it.'

He parked the car outside a restaurant and came around to her side to open her door. As she unfolded herself from the car he took her arm and turned her to look at him. 'Anna…' He tipped up her chin, his expression instantly softening at the moisture clinging to her eyelashes. 'Anna…'

'Don't.' She tried to brush him off but his hold remained immovable.

'Listen to me, *cara*,' he said gently. 'I promise not to mention the past for the rest of tonight. OK?'

'You won't be able to stop yourself,' she said with a sniff.

'Watch me,' he said. 'I will be the perfect partner.'

He led her into the softly lit Italian restaurant and within a few moments they were shown to a table in an intimate corner. He reached for her hand across the table and absently played with her fingers, his eyes never once leaving her face. 'Anna…'

'Yes?'

'Nothing…' He smiled. 'Just Anna.'

'Lucio?'

'Mmm?'

She gently extracted her hand from his and placed it in her lap. 'Why do you want to marry me?'

He looked at her for a long time before answering. 'Sammy needs a father.'

'Is that your only reason?'

'What other reason could there be?' he asked, leaning back in his chair.

'I don't know…but I think it's rather a drastic step to take, considering our…history.'

'I thought the topic of our history was out of bounds for this evening?'

'I know, but I've been thinking…' She lifted her troubled gaze to his. 'This trip to Rome you're planning…Have you considered your family's reaction to the news of your marriage to me?'

'I have considered it.'

'And?'

'And we will marry regardless.'

'But it will be so difficult…with Carlo and…'

'I did not make it difficult, Anna, you did. Carlo will accept you as his sister-in-law because I demand it, so too will the rest of my family.'

'Does your mother know about…?'

'No.' He reached for his wine. 'I thought it best at the time to allow her to think we'd had a lovers' tiff and called off our marriage.'

'Hasn't she ever asked you what went wrong?'

'My mother knows me too well. She understands when a subject is not open for discussion and makes every effort to steer clear of it.'

'And your sister, Giulia?'

'Giulia has always maintained her high regard for you,' he said. 'It might please you to know she berated me for every type of fool for letting you go.'

'And you weren't tempted to tell her the truth?'

'I was very tempted.' His eyes held hers for an infinitesimal pause.

'What stopped you?'

He twirled his wine glass for a moment. 'Carlo felt so guilty about it all I decided it would only make him more uncomfortable to have the rest of the family in on the secret.'

Somehow his answer disappointed her; she sat staring at her fruit juice, hoping he wouldn't see how much.

'Have you ever wanted to tell Jenny the truth?' he asked.

'Sometimes…'

'How did you explain our break-up?'

'I told her we'd fallen out of love,' she said, still avoiding his eyes. 'It was easier that way and, as it turned out, more or less true.'

'Have you been involved with anyone since?' he asked, watching her steadily.

She toyed with her glass with restless fingers. 'Being a single mother is somewhat of a stumbling block to men these days. Most men prefer a woman without baggage.'

'Sammy's a great little kid,' he said.

'Thank you.' She felt her heart swell at his compliment.

A funny little silence fell between them. Anna fidgeted with her napkin and then painstakingly rearranged her cutlery.

'I rang my family last night. I told them Sammy is my child,' he said.

Anna's fork slid out of her grasp to the floor with a noisy clatter. 'Were they…upset?'

'A bit.' He gave a wry grimace. 'My mother was furious with me, of course, and Giulia was livid to think I'd deserted you in your hour of need.'

'It must have been very difficult for you.'

'I was just thinking the very same about you,' he replied. 'How long was it before you found out you were expecting Carlo's child?'

'Too long to do much more than panic,' she admitted. 'I guess I ignored the usual signs as I was so…upset at what had happened. I was nearly three months' pregnant before I realised. It was such a shock. I couldn't tell anyone the truth, which made it a hundred times worse.'

'Did you ever consider getting rid of the pregnancy?'

She jerked upright in her seat and faced him. 'No, I never considered it. It was my mistake…I was prepared to pay for it.'

'On all accounts you paid dearly.'

'I'm surprised you think so,' she put in, 'especially since you've been so busy tailormaking your own revenge.'

'I too was shocked to find you'd had a child,' he confessed. 'For a while there I hoped it was mine, but then I knew it had to be Carlo's as we'd always used protection.'

'I wish he was yours,' she said before she could stop herself.

His eyes went to hers, their dark depths suddenly intense. 'Do you know how much I wish that too? I look at him and see myself. I see what we could have had together.'

'I'm so sorry...'

He drained his glass and put it back down with a heavy thud. 'Not half as sorry as me.'

'I wish I could remember...'

'I wish for once you would stop this nonsense of "not remembering". What will it take for you to accept your role in this? Aren't the photographs enough? What do you want? Eyewitnesses?'

She twisted her napkin into a knot in her lap. 'It would make it so much easier if I could remember what led up to me...being in Carlo's bed.'

'Let me fill in the gaps for you.' His tone was bitter. 'You shared a bottle of champagne with him and when he was a little under the weather you made a pass at him which in his inebriated state he was unable to resist. You and that body of yours pack quite a punch. I don't blame him for taking what was on offer. I would have done the very same.'

Shame coursed through her at his harsh statement.

'But I'm prepared to put that aside now so we can concentrate on the future,' he continued. 'Sammy has a right to his heritage as a Ventressi and I will make sure he gets it.'

'Even if it means tying yourself to a woman you no longer feel anything for?'

His eyes were hard as they meshed with hers. 'I wouldn't go as far as saying I don't feel anything for you; in fact, I feel a great deal. I feel the most consuming anger, for a start, and, when I let my guard down, a mild affection, but to be perfectly honest the primary reason I have for tying myself to you is that I cannot get you out of my system. I want you physically. It is like a gnawing hunger inside me. The fact that you slept with my brother and gave birth to his child hasn't dampened it one little bit. I want you and I will go to any lengths to have you.'

'I can't do it, Lucio.' Her voice was just a whisper of sound. 'I just can't marry you.'

'You can and you will. I will not settle for anything else.'

'How long do you think such a marriage will last?' Desperation crept into her tone but she could do nothing to hold it back.

'It will last for as long as I say.'

'So you will always have the final say?'

'Do you think I would settle for anything else?' he asked. 'You sabotaged my happiness before—I am not giving you another chance.'

'Please don't ask this of me,' she begged him.

'I'm not asking you, Anna—I'm telling you. You will be my wife within a week and I will not take no for an answer.'

'Do you hate me this much?'

His expression was unreadable. 'I have every reason to hate you, Anna. You, of all people, know that.'

There was little she could say in her own defence. He indeed had every right to hate her for she had betrayed him in a way no man would ever wish to be betrayed.

'I just wish that things were different,' she said with a sigh.

'Do you know how many times I have wished the same?' he asked. 'I lie awake at night and think of what might have been; instead, I am faced with what is.'

'I've ruined both of our lives.' Her shoulders slumped. 'One stupid mistake and I ruined both of our lives.'

'We can salvage what is left,' he said. 'I will make sure of it.'

She gave a humourless laugh. 'Yes, and never let a day go past without reminding me of my indiscretion.'

'Once we are married the past will stay where it belongs—in the past.'

'How can I trust you?' she asked. 'You said this evening you wouldn't once mention the past and yet you've spoken of nothing else.'

'I will do my best to forget what happened between you and Carlo. I can't guarantee it will be easy, but I realise for Sammy's sake I will have to try.'

'I don't know how I am going to face your brother...'

'You need have no fear that Carlo would ever be tempted to look at you that way again. He is very much in love with Milana and would do nothing to jeopardise his marriage.'

'You trust Carlo but not me.'

'Of course I trust Carlo,' he said. 'Unlike you, he has always accepted responsibility for his part in what happened that night.'

'Even to the extent of documenting it,' she put in cynically. 'I'm surprised he didn't have a film and sound crew there as well just to make doubly sure you had no other choice but to believe his story.'

There was another awkward pause.

'By the way, he sent me the photographs.' She broke the silence like a thrown rock as it hit the still surface of a pond.

He went very still.

'At first I thought it might have been a letter from you...An apology for not trying to see my side.'

'Did anything accompany the photographs?' he asked.

'Like what?' she asked. 'A confession of how he'd taken advantage of me? That it wasn't my fault, after all?'

The line of his mouth was grim. 'I meant, was there a letter?'

'Oh, there was a letter all right.' Her mouth tightened bitterly. 'It was short and to the point.'

'What did it say?'

'Not much, but I read between the lines to get the general idea.'

'Do you still have a copy of it?'

'No.'

He gave a cynical little smile. 'No, of course not.'

She stared at him incredulously. 'You don't believe me, do you?'

'Why should I?'

'Because I'm telling you the truth! Your brother sent me a note with the photographs, warning me never to contact you or anyone in your family again.'

'Hardly what I'd call a threat,' he said, 'And entirely understandable in the circumstances.'

'And you wonder why I have no faith in our future,' she said with exasperation. 'You refuse to see me as anything more than an immoral tart who couldn't wait until your back was turned to seduce your brother.'

'I have no choice but to believe it, Anna.' His tone sounded jaded. 'But I wish to God I had an alternative, I really do.'

CHAPTER EIGHT

SAMMY was awake and restless when they got back to the hospital. Anna was on edge from her tense dinner with Lucio and felt too overwrought to deal with a recalcitrant child.

'Stop it, Sammy,' she snapped at him as he tried to get out of bed. 'Go back to sleep. You're going home in the morning as soon as Dr Frentalle sees you.'

'But I want to go home now!' he howled, slapping at her hand as it tried to hold him.

'Sammy.' Lucio's firm deep voice brooked no resistance. 'Get back into bed.'

Sammy's face crumpled but he slid back under the covers, his bottom lip wobbling as he did so.

'Good boy.' Lucio smiled and ruffled his dark curls. 'Now, I will read you a story and once that is finished I am going to take Mummy and Auntie Jenny home. We'll be back in the morning to pick you up.'

'But I was—' Anna began but he sent her a warning glance before turning back to Sammy. 'Mummy needs a good night's sleep before you come home tomorrow. The nurses will take special care of you and before you know it you'll be back home among your toys.'

Sammy gave in with good grace and once Lucio's story was over Anna kissed her son goodnight and made her way out of the ward with Jenny as Lucio said his own farewell.

He joined them in the corridor a few moments later. 'He's just about asleep, as indeed you nearly are.' He touched Anna's cheek with one finger.

'I should be with him,' she said.

113

'You are not helping him by overprotecting him.'

'He's a baby, Lucio! Not a teenager.'

'Darling.' He took her arm and for the sake of her sister, who was watching, she had no choice but to suffer his hold. 'You have been here every night for over a week. You're his mother not his martyr.'

'He might need me during the night.'

'So might I,' he said in an undertone, turning so Jenny couldn't read his lips.

Anna felt her face heating and hastily turned away from his compelling gaze.

The drive back to his house was conducted in silence.

Anna could feel her eyelids dropping with every revolution of the tyres on the road, the smooth movement of the car gradually relaxing her tense shoulders, her head moving sideways to find the upholstered comfort of the curved seat…

'Wake up, *cara*.' Lucio's deep velvet voice sounded near her ear.

She jerked upright and her eyes collided with the deep chocolate of his. 'Where's Jenny?' she asked, glancing around.

'She's already gone inside,' he informed her. 'She has work tomorrow and wanted to get an early night.'

She tried to ease herself away from him, her hand searching for the door catch, but before she could locate it one of his hands came over hers and held it still.

'Why are you always trying to get away from me, Anna?' he asked.

'I…I'm not.'

'Yes, you are. Whenever I come close your eyes widen and you shrink away.'

'Maybe I don't like you touching me.'

The edge of his mouth lifted in a little smile. 'Now we

both know that isn't true. You like me touching you…You like it very much.' He traced the end of his forefinger across the upper bow of her mouth before taking it to her bottom lip, the slow, tantalising movement causing her lips to instantly swell with need.

She could scarcely breathe; what little air she managed to scrape past the tight restriction in her throat felt painfully inadequate to fully inflate her lungs.

'Why deny what is between us?' he asked.

'There's nothing between us,' she croaked.

'Is there not?' He took her hand and placed in on the full thrust of his aroused body. 'I would call that something between us, wouldn't you?'

She felt the throb of his body against her hand and her stomach gave a sudden lurch of aching need.

'You want me as much as I want you,' he said. 'I can see it in your eyes, and I can taste it whenever I kiss you.'

'No…'

His mouth came down and hovered just above hers. 'I can feel it in the way your body tenses when I do this.' He trailed a finger across the upper swell of her right breast.

Anna could feel her breast tightening as it strained against the fabric of her bra beneath her cotton shirt, and she clamped her knees together to stop the rise of heat from her traitorous lower body.

'Don't fight it, Anna.' He moved his hand to her knee and prised it away from its twin, his fingers sliding up along her sensitive inner thigh.

Her breath caught in her throat as his fingers came to the shield of lace covering her, her eyes widening in panic as he shifted the tiny slip of fabric to one side.

She sucked in a ragged breath as his finger slid into her warmth, her bones melting as her moist walls contracted around him.

'I can smell the fragrance of your need,' he breathed

against her trembling mouth. 'It makes me want to fill you with my own.'

She slipped lower in the seat, her back now pressed up against the door handle she'd searched for earlier in vain, her legs parting automatically as he increased the movement of his finger to intensify her pleasure.

She was outside of her own body's jurisdiction. He had total control of her, playing her like a virtuoso does a finely tuned instrument, her pleasure rising just like musical scales, higher and higher, sweeter and sweeter.

Her release burst through the tight restraint of her consciousness, spilling over her in waves, leaving her gasping and breathless.

He gave a satisfied smile at her flushed cheeks and dropped a brief hard kiss to her mouth. 'You are unable to stop yourself from responding to me. Is that why you hate me so much, Anna? Because I can reduce you to this?'

She pushed down her skirt and edged away from him, this time finding the door handle and almost tumbling backwards out of the car in her haste to get away from his hateful smile.

She glared at him as he came around from his side of the car. 'Must you always taint every physical encounter with your prejudice about me?' she asked. 'You never miss an opportunity to make me feel cheap.'

'*Cara.*' His voice was a silky drawl as his eyes ran over her suggestively. 'Considering the amount of money I've spent on your son and sister and yourself so far, the very last thing I would call you is cheap.'

Anger rose in her so swiftly and so violently she didn't stop to think of the consequences. Out of the corner of her eye she saw a hammer hanging on the wall along with a collection of other household tools and, before she could stop herself, she reached for it and threw it with all the pent up fury she possessed.

It shattered the rear window of his car and bounced off over the boot, tearing at the paintwork as it rolled and then fell with a metallic clatter to the concrete floor.

She didn't wait to see his reaction. She turned and flew from the garage with a speed she hadn't known she possessed, her eyes blind with angry tears, her heart pounding in panic at what he would do in retaliation.

She made it to the bedroom but there was no key in the door. Spinning around in trepidation, she almost tripped over her stumbling feet as she lunged towards the door of the *en suite* bathroom, wrenching it open and snapping the lock behind her, leaning back against it, her chest heaving, her breath tearing at her throat.

'Open the door, Anna.'

She dragged some air into her lungs and searched the bathroom for something to prop up against the door but there was nothing.

'Open the door, Anna, or I will open it myself.'

She turned and, taking a deep breath, opened the door. 'All right,' she said, lifting her chin in order to meet his eyes. 'Do what you have to do.'

He stood unmoving for a long moment, his dark gaze unwavering.

'Aren't you going to punish me?' she asked when he didn't speak. 'Or what about throwing me to the bed and reminding me just who is boss around here?'

Still he didn't move or speak.

Anna could feel herself cracking under the strain. She hadn't slept properly in days; her nerves were as tight as a drum and her head was pounding with the effort of keeping the tears at bay.

'What are you, man or mouse?' she went on recklessly. 'Don't you want to prove how big and mighty you are? I've been a bad, bad girl. Why don't you...Why don't you...'

She choked on a sob and dropped her head into her hands. 'Why don't you just get it over with?'

Lucio stepped towards her and, putting his hands on her shaking shoulders, pulled her towards him gently, one of his hands leaving her shoulder to rest on the back of her head.

'You have an appalling view of my self-control, *cara*. I am angry—yes, but I realise you are not yourself this evening. What you need is a long soak in a hot bath and a long sleep in a soft bed.'

'I wrecked your car,' she gulped into his chest.

She felt his shrug against her cheek. 'It is a car, it can be repaired.'

She eased herself away from the wall of his body to look up at him. 'Why are you being so nice about this?'

'Am I being nice?'

'You know you are. I was expecting you to…' Her words fell away in her embarrassment.

'What did you expect me to do, Anna?' he asked.

Her teeth captured her bottom lip momentarily. 'I'm not sure…'

'You have no need to be afraid of me. I would not hurt you physically to prove a point.'

'You don't have to, you do a good enough job emotionally,' she said.

'Meaning?'

Her eyes skittered away from his. 'I find it hard to deal with your insults.'

'You are amazingly fragile,' he observed. 'But I wonder why you insist on provoking me when you are so obviously not up to the task of fighting it out with me?'

'I don't want to fight with you. You're the one who keeps derailing my self-respect with your constant harping on about the past.'

'What do you want me to do, Anna?' he asked roughly. 'Forget all about it? Pretend it didn't happen and play at happy families?' He let her go and strode across the room, his hand going to the back of his neck in a rubbing motion as if he were trying to ease a persistent ache. 'I envy your loss of memory,' he continued. 'I wish I didn't have to see you lying there like that with the fingerprints of my brother all over you.'

Anna felt her stomach tighten with renewed anguish. His bitterness she knew she deserved but she wished she could find some way of erasing what had happened so they could make a fresh start.

'Why are you insisting on marrying me if the sight of me disturbs you so much?' she asked.

He turned back to face her, his expression taut. 'You know why.'

Her stomach did a somersault at the glitter of desire she could see in his dark gaze. 'You will soon tire of me, Lucio, and then what will we have? An empty marriage and a chasm of bitterness that will hurt both of us in the end.'

'We will have children.'

'Children who will be traumatised by our mutual dislike,' she said. 'Can you imagine how it would be, living with parents who snipe and snarl at each other all the time?'

'Anna, you are looking for an escape route but I won't give you one. We will be married next week no matter what arguments you throw up. Sammy needs a father and I cannot take you back to Rome as anything other than my wife.'

'Why not? You've had mistresses before, surely one more wouldn't hurt.'

'My family now believes Sammy to be my son. I have responsibilities that have to be faced.'

'You should have told them the truth.'

'What?' He frowned at her. 'That you'd seduced Carlo and had his bastard child?'

She sucked in an angry breath. 'Don't you dare call Sammy a bastard!'

'It's an unfortunate term but nonetheless true. Sammy may not appear to need a father at this young age but he will need a much firmer hand than yours when he's older.'

'You don't think I'm up to the task of being his parent?'

'I did not say that.'

'What are you saying?'

'You cannot hope to give him the sort of life he deserves as a Ventressi. You have no way of providing for him; certainly not as a hotel cleaner or bar maid.'

'I was working as a personal assistant to a corporate lawyer before I had Sammy,' she said. 'They kept the job open for me but I couldn't cope with the long hours and the high cost of child care when Jenny wasn't free. I had no choice but to let it go.'

'You should have contacted me.'

She slapped her forehead in a now-why-didn't-I-think-of-that? gesture. 'For you to do what?'

'I could have sent you money.'

'With conditions attached, no doubt.' The look she gave him was cynical.

'I had thought of contacting you many times,' he said.

She stared at him for a long moment. 'Why?'

He gave one of his could-mean-anything shrugs. 'I wanted to make sure I hadn't made a mistake in letting you go.'

'You obviously quickly overcame the impulse.'

'I was shocked when I heard you had a child,' he said, ignoring her sarcasm. 'For a time I hoped…'

Anna's chest felt tight with emotion at the regret in his tone.

'But I soon assured myself I wasn't responsible,' he continued. 'But then that left the problem of Carlo and whether he should be told. But before I could make up my mind he announced his engagement to Milana. It didn't seem the right time to drop that particular bombshell and as time went on it was even less appropriate to do so.'

'It's never going to be appropriate, is it?' she asked.

'Not now, no. Carlo and Milana are so happy—it would be unforgivable to destroy what they have.'

'So you are prepared to tie yourself into an unhappy union to protect him from the truth?'

'I am prepared to do what it takes to give Sammy the heritage that is rightly his. He has a grandmother he hasn't yet met and uncles and aunts and cousins. He has a right to know who his family is.'

'What about my rights?' she asked. 'Do I have any in this arrangement?'

'You will be well provided for and I will endeavour to be a compassionate husband.'

'That is when you're not angry with me.'

'I am not always angry with you, *cara*.'

'I see it in your eyes,' she said. 'You can hardly bear to look at me at times. Do you think I don't see that?'

'I am not angry with you now.'

'No, but it wouldn't take much to make you so.'

'Perhaps not, but since there are no hammers in this room I think I can safely say I will not lose my temper.'

She turned away from his teasing smile and stomped back towards the bathroom. 'I'm going to have a bath,' she said and slammed the door behind her.

Lucio came back into the bedroom an hour later to find her curled up in the big bed, fast asleep with her still damp hair spread out along the pillow. He sighed and replaced the sheet she'd thrown off, tucking it around her gently, hardly daring to touch her in case his need for her escalated out of control. He had only to look at her to feel the blood surge to his lower body, the ache of desire almost too much to contain.

It annoyed him she had that effect on him, even after all this time. He'd expected to take one look at her and walk away with no regrets but as soon as he'd seen the vulner-ability in her blue gaze all his earlier resolve had melted.

Seeing her making his bed in the hotel suite had changed everything. He knew then he had to have her and he'd been ruthless in bringing about her capitulation even though he still felt some slight residue of guilt. But Sammy was a Ventressi and he could hardly stand by and do nothing. By marrying Anna so many problems would be solved, al-though it would create a few more...

Anna opened her eyes to find Lucio sitting on the edge of the bed, his dark, watchful gaze resting on her.

She brushed a strand of hair out of her eyes with a ner-vous movement of her hand and made to sit up.

'No, stay there,' he said, pressing her back down with one hand on her shoulder. 'I didn't mean to wake you. I was checking to see if you were all right.'

'I'm fine.'

'Can I get you anything?' he asked. 'A drink or some-thing?'

'No...' She ran her tongue over the parchment of her lips. 'I'm not thirsty.'

'Something to eat?'

She shook her head.

'I'll leave you in peace then.' He made to get up but one of her hands reached out and caught his sleeve. He looked down at her with a questioning glance. 'What do you want, Anna?'

She let her hand slide off his sleeve, her cheeks firing with heated colour.

He sat back down on the edge of the bed and turned her averted face back to his. 'Anna? What is it?'

She caught her lip between her teeth and then, letting it

go, took the plunge. 'Why don't you ever stay the whole night with me?'

His eyes held hers for a heart-stopping moment. 'You want me to stay with you?'

'I don't like the way you…you use me and disappear.'

'I do not use you, Anna.'

'But you do disappear,' she said.

'I thought you wanted to rid yourself of my hateful presence?'

'It's not hateful all the time.' She gave her sheet an agitated pluck with her fingers. 'In fact, you can be surprisingly nice at times.'

'Because I overlooked your little outburst earlier?'

'That and other things.'

'What other things?'

She chewed her lip and meticulously avoided his gaze.

'Anna, look at me.' He tilted her chin. 'Do you want me to sleep with you?'

She felt herself drowning in the dark, fathomless pools of his eyes. Her throat closed over as need took hold of her, sending arrows of heat to the centre of her being.

'Answer me.'

'I…' She moistened her lips once more. 'I…want you to stay with me.'

He bent his head to hers and brushed his lips across hers in a tempting caress that made her ache for more. He lifted his head to smile down at her, the burning intensity of his eyes igniting the embers of her desire into hungry, leaping flames.

She grasped at his head and brought it back down to hers with a strength she didn't know she possessed, her fingers burying in the thickness of his dark hair as she pressed her mouth to his.

His tongue came to hers with a rasping thrust as he took control of the kiss with a mastery that delighted her. He leaned his weight over her, pressing her back into the pillows, his chest crushing the softness of her breasts.

She felt the surge of his body through the sheet that still covered her, the barrier of fabric intensifying her need to get even closer.

He broke the kiss to stand up and remove his clothes, his eyes never leaving hers. She watched him as he tossed his shirt aside and heeled himself out of his shoes before reaching for his belt. Her eyes widened as he stepped out of his trousers, the black undershorts stretched by the thickened male flesh.

He tore the sheet off the bed with one intensely masculine movement of his hand. 'You make me mad with desire,' he growled as he came down over her. 'I want to bury myself inside you.'

She sucked in a ragged little breath as he nudged her thighs apart, her inner flesh tingling with anticipation of the urgent glide of his body within hers.

'Tell me to slow down,' he groaned against her mouth.

'I don't want you to slow down.'

'I will hurt you.'

'You won't hurt me,' she gasped as he thrust into her deeply.

He moved within her urgently, carrying her along with him on a raging tide of spiralling desire, his guttural groans of need like music to her ears.

With every surge of his body she felt herself move closer to the highest point of rapture, the entire surface of her skin lifting in tiny goosebumps as each muscle in her body tensed for the final flight into paradise.

She arched her back beneath him, unable to contain the torrent of urgency as it clawed at her to be assuaged. She clutched handfuls of the sheets either side of her, desperate for an anchor in the raging sea of want that was sweeping her away.

He drove her on relentlessly, his breathing hectic, his body slick with fine beads of perspiration as he urged her on.

She felt him fighting for control, felt the tight clench of muscles and the slight decrease in pace as he brought himself back from the brink in an effort to stall his pleasure in order for her to take hers.

She felt herself tipping over the edge in an explosion of sensation, making her feel as if her body had shattered into a thousand tiny pieces, each one free-falling into space, leaving her spent in the tight embrace of his arms.

He gave one last deep groan, his expression above hers contorted with pleasure as he emptied himself, sending aftershocks of delight through her still quivering flesh.

His weight was a blessed burden as he sank with relaxation against her, his head buried into her neck, his breathing still hurried.

She lay in the circle of his arms without moving or speaking, content to feel his warm presence still within her as if he didn't want to break the intimate contact.

She stroked the smooth skin of his back, her fingers moving over the contours of his muscles as if committing them to memory, her thoughts drifting forwards to a time when perhaps memory would be all she would have of him.

The fire of his passion would surely burn itself out and where would she be then? He would secure custody of any children they had, including Sammy, leaving her to a lifetime of lost hopes. Her love for him wasn't a currency he'd be interested in, even if she were to offer it to him. His primary motivation had been revenge for the hurt she'd caused him in the past. But she mustn't let him know just how very successful his plan for revenge had turned out.

She felt him stirring, his weight shifting as he leaned on his elbows to look down at her.

'You look pensive,' he said, brushing a strand of hair off her cheek. 'What are you thinking about?'

'Nothing much.'

'Are you thinking about Carlo?'

She tensed at the seemingly casual question. 'No, of course not.'

'Do you ever think about him?'

'I try not to.'

'He's the father of your child.'

'I don't think of him in that way.'

'What way do you think of him?' he asked.

She felt uncomfortable under his intense scrutiny. 'I don't want to talk about Carlo.'

'You still care for him, don't you?'

'Don't be so ridiculous.' She tried to roll away but he held her beneath him with a strength and purpose that unnerved her.

'Your passionate response to me is a clue, you know,' he said. 'You hate me but you suffer my touch by pretending I'm my brother.'

She gaped at him in shock and outrage. 'I do no such thing!'

'How can I believe you?' he asked. 'You went from my arms to his. How else can I explain it?'

'I don't wish to continue this discussion,' she bit out and tried to free herself again to no avail. 'Let me go, Lucio.'

His rumble of amused laughter was her final undoing.

She freed one hand and swung it at his face with all the force she could put behind it but somehow he avoided it.

'I overlooked the hammer but this I will not excuse,' he said.

'You asked for it!' She glared at him.

'I will not tolerate violence from you.'

'What are you going to do about it?' she threw at him challengingly.

His dark eyes speared hers as the silence lay thick and heavy between them, the intimate throb of his body still encased in hers reminding her of the very uneven playing field she was on.

'Would you like to take a wild guess?' he asked with a subtle movement of his lower body.

'No...' she croaked, her spine weakening and her legs going to mush.

'Then perhaps I should show you instead,' he said and lowered his mouth to hers.

CHAPTER NINE

ANNA woke during the night to find herself in the warm embrace of Lucio's arms, her back curled into his stomach, his masculine hair tickling the sensitive skin of her bottom.

'Can't you sleep?' he rumbled near her ear as one of his hands glided from her waist to cup her breast.

'I...I was asleep,' she said, tensing as his growing erection came between her legs. 'But something woke me.'

He nuzzled on her earlobe and she gave a little shiver of reaction.

'Are you cold?' he asked.

'No.'

'Do you need anything?'

Only you, she said silently. 'No.'

'Go to sleep, Anna.' He pulled her up close, one of his hands on her stomach, the other still on her breast.

'I can't sleep with you touching me like that,' she said after a restless pause.

His hands fell away as he rolled away to the other side of the bed. 'Goodnight, Anna.'

She listened to the sound of his breathing for endless minutes. 'Lucio?'

'Mmm?'

She turned her head to look at him but his back was still towards her. 'Are you asleep?' she whispered.

'I was asleep,' he mumbled into his pillow, 'but someone just woke me.'

'Sorry.'

She heard the bedclothes rustle as he reached for the bed-side lamp, the soft light casting his tanned body into a golden glow. He turned to face her, the sheet slipping to reveal the dark arrow of masculine hair from his navel downwards. 'What's on your mind?' he asked.

'Nothing.' She lowered her gaze.

'Are you worried about Sammy?'

She felt ashamed to admit she hadn't once thought of her son; her mind had been too full of Lucio.

'No, I know he'll be fine. He never usually wakes at night.'

'Then what's troubling you?'

She took a shaky breath and met his eyes. 'I don't think I've ever thanked you properly for what you did for Sammy.'

He gave his pillow a soft punch and lay his head back down. 'Couldn't you have waited until morning to thank me?'

'No...I wanted to do it now.'

He turned his head to the bedside clock. 'It's four a.m., Anna. I won't even remember what you say.'

'I still need to say it even if you don't remember it.'

He shut his eyes and sighed. 'Say it if you must.'

She stared at his still figure for a moment. 'Lucio?'

'Mmm?' He opened one eye as he turned his head on the pillow.

'Thank you.'

'My pleasure. Now go to sleep.'

He reached for the bedside lamp but she counteracted the movement of his arm with a restraining hand on his wrist.

'What it is now?' he asked.

'Thank you for the beautiful clothes you bought Jenny.'

'It was nothing, now—'

'And the toys you bought for Sammy.'

'He deserves them. Now will you please be quiet and go to sleep before I lose my temper?'

'Sorry.' She flung herself to the other side of the bed and

turned her back. The lamp clicked off and she shut her eyes against the tears behind her lashes. Lucio lay staring at the dancing shadows on the ceiling for a full minute. He swore as he jack-knifed upwards to turn on the lamp again. 'Why are you crying?'

'I'm not crying,' she sobbed.

He got out of his side of the bed and came around to where she was buried under the bedclothes.

'Come out from under there and tell me what's going on.'

'I don't want to come out.'

'You'll suffocate under there.'

'What would you care?' she said sniffing.

'Do you have life insurance?'

'No.'

'Then don't do anything drastic until we organise some for you.'

She poked her head out to glare at him. 'You have a sick sense of humour, do you know that?'

'It gets me by.'

'How can you be so flippant?'

'How can you be so serious all the time?' he shot back. 'I've never met anyone as strung up as you.'

'I wouldn't be so strung up if you hadn't taken over my life!'

'Is this about our impending marriage?' he asked.

'You don't really want to marry me,' she said.

'I have every intention of doing so.'

'But for all the wrong reasons!'

'You have only yourself to blame if my reasons for marrying you are not the same as those of four years ago.'

'Here we go again.' She sprang to her feet and flounced to the other side of the room, dragging the sheet with her to cover her nakedness. 'You just can't let it be, can you? Every chance you get you rub my nose in it again. Can't you see how our marriage has no hope? You won't be able to stop yourself from chipping away at me until there's nothing left.'

'I will make you a promise.'

'I can just imagine how long you'll keep it.'

'I will not mention what happened between you and Carlo again.'

'You expect me to believe you'll hold true to that?'

'You have my word.'

She held his look for as long as she could. 'I wish I could believe you.'

'Believe me, Anna. I will not mention it again. It quite clearly causes you distress and it serves no purpose. You appear to be genuinely sorry for what happened.'

'How very insightful of you.'

'The subject is now closed.'

'Until the next time,' she muttered under her breath.

'I mean it, Anna. Now, come back to bed; your eyes are like an owl's. You are like an overtired child who has been allowed to stay up too late.'

She sighed in defeat and came back to the bed. Lucio took the sheet from her and roughly remade the bed before turning back to her. 'Now, in you get and no more talking. We have a big day tomorrow with Sammy coming home and it won't help things if we are both hollow-eyed and tetchy.'

Anna slipped into her side of the bed as Lucio went to his. She felt the depression of the mattress as he lay down, every skin cell of her body crying out for his touch.

'Go to sleep, Anna,' he said softly.

She turned over and shut her eyes but she felt restless and on edge and opened them again. Her legs felt twitchy and her hands ached to reach out to the long, silent figure beside her. She wanted to feel the silk of his skin along his back, to scrape her fingers over his chest hair, to feel the hard, flat male nipples, to let her hand slip lower and lower until she came to his…

The lamp clicked on, startling her out of her sensual reverie.

'*Dio!*' Lucio swore.

'What's wrong?' she asked, turning to look at him.

His eyes were lustrous with desire as he reached for her, pulling her roughly into his arms, his long legs wrapping around hers.

'You are driving me crazy, *cara*,' he growled deep in his throat.

'I…I am?' She blinked at him.

'You know you are.' His mouth touched the corner of hers. 'I can't lie next to you without touching you.'

'I didn't mean to disturb you.' She traced a circle around his right nipple with the tip of her index finger.

'Did you not?' His mouth tilted in a sensuous smile.

'No…'

He pressed her down and came over her with his weight, his mouth just above hers. 'You disturb me a very great deal, Anna.'

'I do?'

He moved against her and she gasped at the hard ridge of his arousal seeking her body's warmth.

'See how much you disturb me?' he said, driving himself forward into her moistness.

'Oh…Oh…' She bit down on her lip, her fingers digging into his shoulders to hold herself steady under the passionate onslaught of his powerful body.

She was slipping into a sea of sensuality, waves rolling over her as she rode the tide of longing that rose in her fevered blood. She couldn't hold back, couldn't stem the rush of feeling that charged through her with every deep stroke of his maleness within her. Her inner body tightened around him while her limbs went to jelly and her spine loosened with the ache of pressing need.

His hungry mouth fed on hers, the stab and withdrawal movements of his tongue mimicking the movement of his body in the tight cocoon of hers. She could feel his struggle to maintain control and it secretly delighted her. The sense of feminine power was overwhelming to her—he wanted her even though he had cut her from his life all those years ago. His bitterness over her past betrayal was secondary to his all-consuming need of her. She felt that driving need as he increased his pace, sweeping her along with it in a maelstrom of wild feelings—wild, out of control and desperate feelings of insatiable desire.

She was spinning inside her head, a million sparks exploding in her brain as he drove her to paradise with his body and his hands, leaving her shaking and shuddering beneath his masterful touch.

She was still floating as he expelled himself, his weight collapsing on her as the relaxation of his release stole the strength from his limbs. His chest rose and fell against hers, the fine sheen of sweat between their bodies like satin, and the soft scent of their lovemaking in the air like an intoxicating drug. Anna felt her eyelids drifting down, her body totally relaxed in his warm embrace.

Lucio lifted his head a few minutes later and looked down at her lying at ease in his arms, her legs still entwined with his, her body holding him intimately, damply…sexily…

The sigh he gave hitched in his throat before travelling down to his belly, feeling more like a pain than a movement of air.

He picked up a loose strand of her hair off her face and tucked it gently behind the shell of her left ear before lowering his mouth to the soft bow of hers, pressing a barely there kiss on her lips.

She sighed and murmured his name. 'Lucio?'

'Yes, Anna?' he breathed.

She gave another childlike sigh and snuggled her head sideways into the pillow. 'Nothing…just Lucio…'

A small, rueful smile lifted the edges of his mouth as he watched the soft rise and fall of her breathing. She was finally asleep after keeping him awake for hours and, tired as he was, he knew with her lying like that in his arms, sleep for him was now even further away.

Sammy was full of high spirits as soon as he came home from hospital, determined to play with every toy Lucio had bought for him. Anna had to put the brakes on him more than once, terrified he'd undo all the good Dr Frentalle had done but fortunately he survived till nightfall when he fell into an exhausted but contented sleep.

Anna had not long tucked him in when Lucio appeared in the doorway of Sammy's room. 'Out for the count?' he asked.

She nodded and, joining him at the door, gently pulled it half shut behind her. 'He was full of beans but by teatime he started to flag, thank goodness.'

He fell into step with her as they made their way downstairs. 'Jenny had a good day at the office,' he informed her. 'She was very efficient, or so my secretary said. Did heaps of filing for her and ran some errands.'

Anna smiled. 'Jenny told me she had a great day. Thank you for giving her the opportunity.'

He shrugged off her thanks and shouldered open the lounge door, indicating for her to precede him. 'She loved it so much she decided to stay here and work while we go to Italy.'

She turned to look at him, her expression worried. 'Are you sure that's wise? She's only nineteen and—'

'She'll be fine; anyway, Rosa will be here to take care of the house and any of her needs.'

'But what if she needs me or—'

Lucio pressed the tip of one finger against her lips to stall her protest. 'Anna, you are her sister, not her mother. She is well and truly old enough to spend a month here with my housekeeper. Now, sit down and tell me all about your day while I organise us both a drink.'

Anna sat and filled him in on Sammy's antics, relieved she had something to talk about other than their relationship and impending marriage. She even discussed the weather at one point rather than mention their future, even though it loomed large in her tortured mind.

Four years ago marriage to Lucio had been her most joyful dream, their love and mutual passion promising them a blissful life together. Her night of betrayal had destroyed that dream, but now four years on he wanted her to marry him in spite of it.

If she didn't still love him, her choice would have been so much easier, but her love bound her to him as firmly as any golden band.

His obvious attachment to Sammy was of immense comfort to her. It showed her what sort of man he really was, that he could put aside his own prejudice and bitterness and relate to her little son for the endearing toddler he was and not just as the bastard child of his brother.

As for his feelings for her—they were still a mystery. He'd mentioned that he felt a mild affection for her when he wasn't angry with her, but how long that would last was anyone's guess. He was unlikely to forget how she'd hurt him even though he'd promised he'd never refer to it again. It was like a nasty wound roughly covered by an inadequate bandage; eventually the infection would seep through to the surface, staining their lives once more.

Marriage to Lucio would take both strength and courage, but her training ground as the single parent of a desperately ill child surely had honed those qualities into her personality? She could be both strong and courageous, but then she would need to be in order to keep the truth of her feelings under wraps for the sake of her pride. To tell him of how she had never stopped loving him would surely be emotional suicide.

'Where is Jenny?' Anna took a break from the subject of the weather to ask.

Lucio took a long swallow of his brandy before replying. 'She's gone on a date.'

'*A date?*' Anna sprang to her feet in agitation. 'What sort of date?'

'The usual sort, a boy and a girl, a movie or dinner—that sort of thing.'

'That sort of thing usually leads to trouble!'

'Relax, Anna. Romeo is a nice young man who—'

'*Romeo?*' She frowned.

'It's a good Italian name.'

'That's not the point.' She let out her breath. 'Jenny has no experience with the Romeos of this world.'

'Romeo Benetto is a junior accountant in my company. He has impeccable manners and will take great care of your sister.'

'He's Italian.'

'So?' He gave her a hard look.

'I don't trust Italian men.'

'What a pity, since within days you will be marrying one.'

'I might not go through with it.' She lifted her chin.

He twirled the glass in his hands in such a contemplative action a tiny *frisson* of trepidation scuttled up Anna's spinal cord.

'Then I shall have to think of a way to ensure you do go through with it.'

'The bills are already paid for Sammy's surgery,' she

pointed out. 'There isn't anything else you can hang over my head to force me.'

'Isn't there?' The cold darkness of his eyes suddenly chilled her.

She swallowed the lump of fear in her throat and stilled the restlessness of her fluttering hands by balling them into fists at her sides. 'No,' she said with far more confidence than she felt.

'There is that trying little matter of my car.' His tone was deceptively calm.

'Y…your car?' She swallowed again.

'I'm sure you know the one?' He gave her a little unreadable smile. 'Not the one Guido used today to take you to pick up Sammy, but the other one.'

She felt the moisture building in her tightly clenched hands and opened them to release it against the fabric of her pants.

'Yes, *cara*, the one with the hammer still lying on the back seat surrounded by shattered glass. A hammer, I might mention at this point, which still has your fingerprints all over it.'

Anna's heart thumped at the back of her sternum until she was sure it was going to come right through. She opened her mouth to speak but no sound came out.

'It would take just one phone call to the police to report an incident of wilful damage to property to make the task of removing Sammy from your custody as easy as…What shall we say? Child's play?'

'You bastard!' her voice spewed out on a harsh breath.

He gave her an imperious look. 'You think I won't do it?'

She *knew* he would do it. She'd played right into his hands by being so impulsive and now he had her right where he wanted her—in his total control.

'No wonder you were being so nice about it!' she spat at

him. 'You were busily planning your little pay-back with your usual cunning and precision.'

'Ah, but you are so delightfully cooperative,' he drawled. 'You have such a volatile temper…so little self-control.'

She could barely see for the red spots of anger before her flashing blue eyes. She fought to contain it but it rose like a flood behind paper floodgates, bursting through with tearing, devastating force.

She flung herself at him, fists flailing at his chest and anywhere she could reach him.

He held her off with one strong outstretched arm, his expression rigidly composed, making her wild outburst seem all the more excessive.

'You want to fight dirty, Anna?' His breathing was heavy as he secured one of her escaping hands. She gritted her teeth and tried to move but she came into contact with his rock-hard arousal and sank down as far as she could on to the sofa behind them.

He could still reach her there, the heat and probe of his body burning her into an unwilling submission. 'Go on,' he challenged her. 'Fight me. I think we'll both enjoy it.'

'Go to hell!' she said, but he thrust himself down next to her.

She couldn't quite stifle her gasp as his body surged against her, the barrier of her clothes hardly taking away from the pleasure of the contact. 'I hate you!' She struggled wildly but she knew it was herself she was fighting, not him.

He held her gently and with ease even though his breathing was hurried and his body hard and pulsing. 'I don't care what you feel for me as long as your body welcomes me the way it is welcoming me.'

She wanted to deny it even as her pelvis rose to meet the downward thrust of his.

He tugged at her pants and dragged them from her hips

before releasing himself from his own, still with one hand holding both her hands above her head.

'Tell me if you want me to stop,' he growled as his mouth came down over hers.

His kiss was deep and commanding and she felt herself slipping into its seductive vortex with each flick of his tongue against hers.

Stopping wasn't an option any more. He entered her slickly and deeply.

She was on an upward spiral to a height he held out to her like a prize, a prize she wanted to grab with both hands and everything that was within her. Her body tingled and tensed, tightened and stretched, her mind gradually whirling away from consciousness as the tension grew to bursting point.

His pace increased with her breathy gasps of delight as his body coaxed her closer and closer, each deep thrust sending sparks of feeling through her hectic bloodstream.

Finally she was there with a cascading shower of fragmented colour inside her head, her quivering body shivering out its release as his prepared itself for the final explosion of feeling.

She felt him burst forth from the tight banks of restraint, his warmth filling her, anointing her with the milk of life, his breathing ragged as the last deep, satisfied groan left his lips.

Anna kept very still as shame coloured her from head to foot. She clamped her eyes shut as she mentally berated herself for her weakness. No wonder he thought her a wanton temptress, the way she fell into his arms even as she tried to deny her attraction. No wonder he thought her the perpetrator of his brother's downfall.

Lucio had only to touch her and her body ignited into a raging inferno. Why wouldn't he assume his brother had experienced the same?

Lucio rolled away in one movement and got to his feet, rearranging his trousers without once looking her way.

Some vestige of pride made her swing her legs over the edge of the sofa with the same casualness and reposition her own clothing, even though she felt as if the only proper place for her was under the rug beneath her feet.

She felt his tension, however, in the way he avoided her eyes by inspecting the view from the windows, his back turned to her, his shoulders stiff, his legs slightly apart, his hands thrust into his trouser pockets.

'We will be married in three days' time,' he announced, as if commenting on the heat haze outside the window. 'I will accept no refusals on your part.'

'I don't suppose you want me to wear white or a veil?'

He turned and gave her a raking look. 'You can if you like but we both know what you are and no amount of white is going to be able to disguise it.'

He turned and left the room, the lounge door swinging shut behind him, locking her inside the room with his hateful words still ringing in the air.

CHAPTER TEN

THE day of the wedding saw the sky split with green-tinged flashes of lightning closely followed by bellowing thunder interspersed with torrential rain. Anna couldn't help feeling it was some sort of omen for the future she was committing herself to.

If the last few days had been any indication, it wasn't going to be a match made in heaven. Lucio had kept his distance ever since the night she'd lost her temper, choosing to sleep elsewhere, and if pressed to converse with her only did so in clipped, distant tones. In the presence of Sammy and Jenny he resumed his easygoing self, which only added to Anna's feelings of despair. She knew he was angry with her and to some degree felt it was justified, but she couldn't help wishing things were different.

The ceremony was brief and impersonal, nothing like the gala affair she and Jenny had planned four years ago whilst in Rome.

She stood in front of the marriage celebrant and articulated her vows in a strangled voice and wondered if the crashing lightning and thunder above her head was retribution from some metaphysical being who was frowning on her for her past sins.

Lucio seemed to be suffering no such misgivings as he placed the ring on her hand and gave her what only could be described as a perfunctory kiss for the benefit of the small gathering of witnesses, including a rapturous Jenny and a bug-eyed Sammy.

The reception was hardly worthy of the name unless one counted a few glasses of French champagne and a tray of unrecognisable hors d'oeuvres in a plush hotel foyer with a passable pianist doing his best to play his way through what appeared to be a very limited repertoire.

Anna was glad when the pretence was over so they could high-tail it out of there back to Lucio's house where at least she knew where she stood.

Sammy went to bed without his usual fuss and Jenny gave a shy smile as the doorbell rang announcing her equally shy suitor. Anna waved them off at the door and turned to make her way upstairs when Lucio's voice stalled her.

'Anna.'

'Yes?' She gave him a dismissive glance.

His eyes met hers across the hall and she unconsciously tightened her hands by her sides.

'I want to discuss something with you,' he said.

'It's a bit late for a pre-nuptial agreement,' she quipped.

His mouth tightened and she felt a perverse sort of satisfaction at noticing his hands had also balled into fists. 'We leave for Rome in three weeks,' he said.

'It's a little early to pack,' she said. 'Was there anything else?'

She heard his indrawn breath and mentally scratched up another point in her favour.

'We can discuss this out here in the hall or in the lounge. What would you prefer?' His tone was clipped.

She set her chin at a defiant angle and placed her right foot on the first step of the staircase. 'I would prefer it if you would allow me to go to bed. I don't feel in the mood for a post-mortem on our wedding, to use the term in its loosest sense.'

'Meaning?' One dark brow raised over one equally dark eye.

'It was hardly what one could call a wedding, wouldn't you agree? A bride blackmailed to be there and a groom who had nothing but revenge on his mind.'

'I can assure you, Anna, revenge was not the only thing on my mind.'

'Oh, really?' She gave him an arctic look. 'Well I have nothing on my mind but sleep.' She took three steps up the staircase when his deep voice stalled her.

'I could change your mind.'

She took a breath and turned back to face him with a scathing glance. 'What with?'

'You know what with.'

The breath she sucked in hurt damnably but she hoped he didn't see it. She looked down her nose at him and reached for the banister once more but a sudden deep pain hit her in the middle of her belly and she almost folded with the impact.

'Oh…God…' She stumbled and grasped at the railing with useless fingers.

'Anna!' Lucio's voice tore from his throat as he lunged up the stairs to her sagging form. 'What's wrong?'

She clawed at the banister as if it were her only lifeline, her face draining of all colour. 'I…I don't know…'

He hauled her to her unsteady feet and, scooping her up into his arms, carried her up the stairs to the master bedroom. Anna considered struggling on principle but the pain was intensifying and she was almost certain she could feel something sticky and wet between her legs.

Lucio laid her on the bed and stood back to inspect her pallid features. 'You look as white as a sheet. I'm calling a doctor.'

She curled into a ball to try to control the pain, her breathing ragged as she fought against crying out.

'What's your doctor's name?' His voice held a trace of panic she'd never heard in it before.

She told him through her clenched teeth and rolled into a tighter ball and bit down on her lip.

She heard him swearing at the person on the other end

of the line. 'This is an emergency! My…my wife is in pain! I don't care how many people need an ambulance right now! I tell you, I will—'

'Oh!' Anna groaned and clutched at her womb with both hands.

Lucio dropped the phone and flew to her side, brushing the damp hair out of her face with a hand that was visibly trembling.

'Anna!'

'I'm bleeding, Lucio…' she gasped.

'What?' He frowned for a moment before comprehension dawned. His tortured gaze travelled to where she had her slim legs tightly clamped together, the seeping stain on the bed linen making his eyes widen in shock.

'You are having a period?'

Oh, I wish! she thought. She clenched her teeth and rode out another contraction of her womb as it expelled its contents.

He sprang to his feet and, wrenching open the door of the *en suite* bathroom, scooped up a towel and came back to her and placed it gently between her legs. 'Is it usually this bad?' he asked, holding the towel in place.

She shook her head and gasped as another knife of pain stabbed her viciously. 'No…I've…I've never had this before…Oh!'

He grabbed the phone and redialed emergency, this time making it clear he wasn't taking no for an answer. Within minutes the screech of a siren in the street announced the arrival of the ambulance, closely followed by a worried Rosa, summoned by an almost incoherent call from her employer.

'I will take care of Sammy for you,' Rosa assured Anna as the paramedics loaded her on the stretcher.

Anna grasped her hand. 'Thank you.'

Lucio virtually shoved his housekeeper away to take command of his wife's loading into the back of the ambulance.

'Careful! You are bumping her!' he growled as the stretcher clattered noisily.

'We're doing our best, mate,' the red-haired paramedic told him with a reassuring smile. 'She'll be fine. Looks like a straightforward miscarriage. Her blood pressure is fine, her pain manageable. She'll be over it before you know it.'

Lucio froze.

A miscarriage?

A baby?

Whose baby?

His?

He stumbled into the back of the vehicle with his thoughts going all over the place as he looked down at the ghostly features of his new wife.

'Anna…'

She reached for his hand and gave it a weak squeeze. 'Sorry.'

'What are you apologising for?' He held her hand as gently as he could, frightened he would harm her.

'I should've told you…'

'Told me what?'

'I was on a low-dose pill, but I hadn't been taking them regularly.'

He sucked in a painful breath that scalded his lungs.

'I didn't think it would happen…' she said in a small voice.

He found it hard to speak. 'Don't worry about it…'

She started to cry and his stomach clenched. 'Anna…it's my fault.'

'No…'

'Shh,' He pressed his fingertip to her mouth before capturing an escaping tear with the pad of his thumb. 'Don't cry, *cara*. Please don't cry…'

* * *

The hospital was noisy and crowded but Lucio's towering presence saw Anna wheeled into a cubicle almost immediately. A senior consultant was summoned and within minutes had organised an operating theatre for a dilatation and curettage to be performed as soon as the anaesthetist arrived.

'Since it's an early miscarriage your wife will recover quite quickly physically,' the doctor reassured Lucio as a junior registrar attended to Anna. 'A few days' rest and she'll be fine, although keep a watch on her emotional health. Many women have difficulty dealing with the loss of a pregnancy, but with a bit of tender handling most recover their spirits soon enough.'

Lucio swallowed convulsively, guilt coursing through him. He wondered what the doctor would think if he told him the way he'd been handling her so far. His feelings for her were as tender and loving as ever could be. The only trouble was that he hadn't wanted to reveal them to her, preferring to put up a self-protective wall of bitterness instead.

He had been totally gutted by her betrayal. Never had he felt so devastated as when he found the one woman he had thought he could trust with his life had seduced his brother in a weak moment, her so-out-of-character actions making it all the harder for him to deal with.

The truth was he hadn't dealt with it, not really. He'd promised her he would no longer refer to it but it still lay festering inside him, niggling at him relentlessly like a pustular sore.

The doctor wrote some notes on a clipboard and handed it to the hovering nurse before turning back to Lucio. 'I heard this is your wedding day.' He gave him an empathetic look. 'Not the best way to start a marriage.'

'Tell me about it.' Lucio's tone was dry.

*   *   *

Anna woke in a fuzzy, disoriented haze, her body feeling sore but without the stabbing cramps of earlier. She turned her head to find Lucio sitting beside her bed with his head in his hands.

As if he felt her gaze he lifted his head and she was shocked by the haggard look to his normally impeccably groomed features. His hair was dishevelled, his jaw dark with stubble and his eyes horribly bloodshot.

'Anna…' She saw his throat move up and down in a deep swallow as he reached for her hands.

'Is…is Sammy all right?' she whispered through her dry throat.

'I called Rosa and Jenny a while ago. He's fine, had his breakfast and was nagging Jenny to take him to the park.'

A small smile tugged at her mouth. 'You look terrible.'

'You should feel it from my side.' He grimaced.

'You look like you haven't slept.'

'I haven't.'

She looked down at their interlaced hands, his long fingers curling around hers, the golden band of their wedding rings shining in unison.

'You scared the hell out of me,' he said after a little silence.

Her eyes lifted to his. 'I'm sorry…I didn't even know I was pregnant. What with all the worry with Sammy, I got out of the routine of taking my pills and, as for my cycle, I had no idea where I was.'

'I should have protected you,' he said heavily. 'I had no right to insist on a physical relationship without taking on that responsibility.'

She lowered her eyes to their hands once more. 'It doesn't matter…'

'Of course it matters! None of this would have happened if I hadn't been so heavy-handed with you.' He dropped her hands and swung away to the end of the bed to look back at her. 'Do you know how much I blame myself for what you've just gone through?'

Anna stared at his ravaged features, her throat closing over. 'It's not your fault.'

His expression grew savage with self-disdain. 'It is my fault. I've done nothing but harangue you from day one. You were under intolerable stress with Sammy and not satisfied that I came on to the scene with my outrageous demands.' He gave her an agonised look and added, 'I was too cruel to you the other night. Do you know how much I hate myself for that?'

'No!' she gasped. 'You weren't…that bad.'

'Wasn't I?' He gave her a pointed look. 'I threatened to call the police about the damage to my car but really you would have been better to have thrown that hammer at my head.'

'I missed.'

A reluctant smile hijacked his mouth. 'You really were going to throw it at me?'

'The car got in the way.' She gave him an answering smile.

He took her hands once more and gave them a gentle squeeze. 'Forgive me, Anna—' his voice was husky and deep '—please say you'll forgive me for what I've done.'

'There's nothing to forgive,' she said, looking away from the intensity of his dark gaze.

'You are too generous.'

'Not at all,' she said. 'Everyone makes mistakes.'

She felt the tightening of his hands on hers as a stretching silence throbbed between them.

He let her hands go and moved back to the end of the bed. 'You are right, of course. How timely to remind me of it. You made one mistake and I have punished you for years, ruining my own life in an attempt to bring about the revenge I thought was most appropriate.'

She felt herself edging closer and closer to tears, his rueful admission tearing at her emotionally. He felt remorse but not love. His guilt would bind them now, not his love.

'Lucio…I…'

'No,' he said, interrupting her. 'Let me finish. We are married now and I can't undo that in the immediate future.'

Her heart squeezed painfully at the bitter resignation on his face.

'I know it's a lot to ask of you but I still would like you and Sammy to travel with me to Rome in three weeks' time. My mother would love to see her grandson and Giulia would, of course, enjoy seeing you once more.'

'And after that?' she asked, her breath tight in her throat. 'What happens when we get back to Australia?'

He gave her a long, unreadable look. 'After that we will separate. I will allow you your freedom which I should never have taken away from you in the first place. I will, of course, make sure you and Sammy are well provided for.'

She didn't want his money! Emotion clogged her throat and her eyes sprouted with moisture.

Lucio's gaze honed in on the brightness of her eyes and his mouth stretched into a thin white embittered line. 'I can see the relief in your eyes. How you must be counting the days until this is over.'

He turned for the door and it swung shut behind him, closing off the whispered sound that escaped from Anna's trembling lips. 'Lucio…'

Anna found the next three weeks almost unbearable. Although Lucio treated her with exceptional politeness and even gentleness if the occasion arose, she knew he was probably ticking off the days when the pretence of their relationship would finally be over.

Jenny was preoccupied with her charming beau and Sammy was enjoying living in a huge house with wall-to-wall television and every toy he had ever dreamed of.

Anna, however, felt increasingly lonely and isolated. Lucio had taken up residence in one of the spare rooms, leaving her to the cavernous loneliness of the master bedroom. He went to work early and came home late, citing on the occasions when she was still up that things were extremely busy at the office.

Of course she didn't believe him.

She felt so increasingly frustrated by his coolness she deliberately waited up for him a couple of evenings before they were to leave for Rome. He came into the lounge close to midnight, his shirt undone and his jacket over one shoulder and his tie loosened. He didn't see her at first and she thought he almost started when she rose from the sofa.

'Lucio.'

'Anna.' He tossed his jacket over the back of a chair and reached for a glass. 'Fancy a drink?' he asked without looking at her.

'No, thank you.'

'Why are you still up?' He raised the glass to his lips and took a deep draught, holding it in his mouth for a moment before swallowing.

'I wanted to talk to you.'

'What about?' He took another mouthful.

She compressed her lips together, her earlier determination to speak with him sagging in the face of his distant demeanour. 'I was wondering what accommodation arrangements had been made for our time in Rome,' she began.

'We will be staying with my mother. My house is being let out currently.' He turned to refill his glass before adding, 'Don't look so worried, Anna. I have told my mother about your miscarriage. She will provide separate rooms for us in order for you to convalesce in peace.'

'I didn't think—'

'No, but my mother did. She already thinks I am a callous brute who should be horsewhipped for my treatment of you.'

'You should have told her the truth.'

'What? That I intend to divorce you as soon as we return to Melbourne? My mother is a devout Catholic—she would be horrified.'

'You'll have to tell her eventually,' she pointed out.

'In my own good time,' he answered and drained his glass.

Anna gnawed at her bottom lip as she watched him refill his glass. 'I've never seen you drink so much before,' she said.

He gave her a glassy-eyed glare. 'Do you have a problem with me drinking?'

'No...I just thought—'

'Don't think, Anna. It doesn't change things one little bit.'

'Are you angry with me?'

'Why would I be angry with you?' he asked. 'You creep around this house, hardly daring to speak in case I snap your head off. Of course I'm not angry.'

'I don't creep around the house.' She defended herself with renewed courage. 'I just got the feeling you'd rather I stayed out of your way. You never come home, you don't...you don't...share our room or—'

'Now that would be taking things way too far, don't you think, Anna? You're surely not offering yourself to me, are you?'

She stared at him for a speechless moment.

His eyes burned down into hers and the heightened colour on his cheekbones warned her he wasn't in the right frame of mind to discuss things rationally.

'You've had too much to drink,' she stated baldly.

'What if I have?' His lip curled in a sneer. 'What are you going to do about it, my sweet little wife?'

She clamped her lips together on a stinging retort and turned to leave but one of his hands caught her and spun her back around to face him.

'Not so fast, Anna.'

'Let me go, Lucio.'

'I don't want to let you go.' His eyes were feverish. 'I never want to let you go.'

She tried to pull out of his hold but his head was already coming down, his mouth so close to hers she had no choice but to shut her eyes against the glint of hatred in his.

His lips crushed hers as his hands tightened on her upper arms to bring her closer into his body, the hard ridge of his arousal a heady reminder of how out of control he already was.

She tasted the fire of cognac on his tongue as it drove through the cleft of her lips in search of hers, its commanding presence mimicking the probe of his maleness against her trembling softness. She felt herself weakening with the flood of desire as it stormed through her, sending the blood thundering through her veins. Her breasts were jammed up against him, her nipples puckering at the feel of his hard muscled chest burning into hers.

He eased her backwards until they were on the sofa in a tangle of legs and arms, his mouth still on hers, hungrily, greedily, passionately.

She heard him groan as her hands went to his waistband, and felt him tense as she freed him, her small fingers shaping his potent length boldly, brazenly.

'I'm not going to last if you do that.' He sucked in a ragged breath.

His agonised confession thrilled her and her fingers moved with even greater purpose, her stomach free-falling at the sound of his pleasure at her touch.

He dragged her hand away and pressed her back into the sofa, tugging at her clothes until she was free, naked and silky with need below him.

His fingers traced her gently, almost reverently, as if she were a precious orchid in his large hand. She could hardly breathe when he slid one finger inside her, stilling his movements until she accepted him further.

She was becoming mindless with her desire for more. His finger wasn't enough, not when she'd already known his full length and strength. Her body ached for his possession, a hollow ache that made her arch herself towards him.

'Please…' she begged unashamedly, her hands clawing at him frantically.

'No, *cara*.' He began to pull away. 'I told myself I wouldn't do this.'

'No!' She clutched at his retreating shoulders in desperation.

He unhooked both of her hands with ease and stood up, his body still rampantly aroused, his dark eyes bright with unrelieved desire, but his jaw equally determined not to give in to it.

He threw her his jacket and turned away, his breathing still laboured. 'Cover yourself and go to bed, Anna.'

She stared at the rigid wall of his back, shame at his rough rejection flowing through her like a red tide.

'But I—'

'Do not argue with me, Anna.' His voice was harsh and she heard the chink of glass against the cognac decanter.

She ignored her scattered clothes to slip her arms through his suit jacket, the fragrance of his aftershave and individual male scent overwhelming her as she clutched it around her shivering body.

'Lucio…' His name escaped her lips on the back of a choked sob.

'Get out, damn you!' He swung around to glare at her,

the glass in his hand nearly cracking in his white-knuckled grip.

She flinched at the obduracy of his tone, her chin wobbling with the effort of keeping control of her disintegrating emotions. 'D…did I do something wrong?' Her voice came out as a thread-like whisper. She watched as he fought with himself, the taut line of his mouth indicating the fragile control he was only just maintaining.

'You seem to be having some difficulty understanding me,' he said through stiff lips.

She ran her tongue over the tombstone dryness of her lips but didn't respond.

'I asked you to leave the room,' he said.

'I know you did.'

'Then it would be in your interests to leave.'

'I'm not frightened of you, Lucio,' she said quietly.

He gave her a malevolent look. 'You are a fool to witness me in this mood.'

'I've seen you in worse.'

'I doubt it.' He put his glass down with an unsteady hand and ran his hand through his hair. 'You weren't there when I saw the photos.'

'You promised not to mention—'

'I know what I promised!' He slammed his hand down on the sideboard.

She bit her lip to stop it from trembling, determined to stand her ground with him, even though it was costing her dearly.

His eyes glittered as they held hers. 'You are asking for trouble to be in the same room as me, Anna. I am not in control of myself and you are likely to suffer the consequences of that lack of control.'

'Why are you doing this to yourself?' she asked, indicating the cognac decanter and his glass.

'I am drowning my sorrows; isn't that how you say it in English?'

'What are you sorrowful about?' She held her breath for his answer.

His shoulders moved up and down as he gave a heavy sigh and his hand reached out for the decanter once more.

'I was a fool to come after you,' he said, refilling his glass. 'I thought I could make you pay but in the end I am the one paying.'

'How are you paying?'

He drank half the glass before answering in a slurred voice. 'What we once had is well and truly dead, Anna. It is time we both accepted it. It is dead.' He drained the glass and set it down with a definitive crack on the sideboard and before she could think of a single thing to say he turned and left the room.

CHAPTER ELEVEN

THE flight to Rome was made all the easier for Anna by the presence of Sammy, who sat between them in unabated excitement in business class. With his constant chatter she was relieved of the task of filling the awkward silences between herself and Lucio who, apart from his affectionate interactions with Sammy, mostly ignored her.

Once Sammy's eyelids drooped Anna tucked him into the generous seat and turned to the movie she'd selected on the console, her eyes staring fixedly on the small screen in front of her but seeing nothing and hearing even less. She was so conscious of Lucio one seat away, his hand around a drink, his gaze focused on a documentary on his own screen.

They had barely spoken in the last two days. Even Jenny had commented on the cold war with a concerned look in her eyes. Anna had smiled and done her best to reassure her that things were fine but she knew she hadn't been all that convincing. The truth was that the clock was ticking on their marriage and she felt each and every passing second like a hammer blow to her heart.

The Leonardo Da Vinci airport in Rome was seething with milling crowds waiting for the arrival of their loved ones, amongst them Jovanna, Lucio's mother, and Giulia, his sister, with her three young children in tow.

'Anna.' Jovanna enveloped her in a warm embrace, kissing both her cheeks and holding her from her with tears in her eyes. 'You have finally returned and where is my precious grandson? Oh!' She put both hands to her cheeks in delight as Sammy appeared from behind the screen of Lucio's long legs. 'But he is the very image of you at that age, Lucio!' she crowed and scooped Sammy up into her arms.

Giulia kissed Anna warmly and introduced her children, her twin two-year-old daughters, Pia and Paola, and her infant son, Antonio, who cooed up at Anna with a gummy smile.

'They're beautiful,' she said, tickling the baby under his chubby chin.

Giulia's expression clouded over as she touched Anna on the arm. 'I am so sorry for your recent loss.'

'Thank you.' Anna lowered her gaze uncomfortably.

'You will soon have another,' Giulia reassured her. 'Maybe one made in Rome, eh?'

Anna wished she could crawl underneath the baggage carrier. How shocked would Giulia be to hear the truth about her brother's relationship with her!

The drive back to Jovanna's house was full of poignant memories for Anna. As they drove past the majestic ruins of the Colosseum she couldn't help recalling the way Lucio had taken her and Jenny on a tour before moving on to the green slopes of the Celian Hill, his easygoing manner so different from the distant and cold figure who sat in a stony silence whenever they were alone.

Sammy was showing clear signs of exhaustion by the time they arrived at Jovanna's palatial home and after a bout of temper-driven tears was packed off to bed with a doting grandmother singing to him to soothe him.

Giulia had left with her children after a promise to return the next day for a family meal, a gathering, Anna assumed with nervous dread, which would include Carlo and his expectant wife.

Lucio came into the lushly appointed sitting room where Anna was sitting on the edge of a sofa, her hands around a glass of orange juice.

'My mother is in raptures over your son,' he said, pouring himself a drink.

'Yes…' She bent her head to her glass, staring at the rim of pith with sightless eyes.

'You have made her very happy,' he added, turning to face her. 'She had more or less given up on me having a child.'

'But he's not your son,' she felt compelled to point out even though it pained her unbearably to do so.

'No.' He took a sip of his drink and set the glass down once more. 'But she doesn't need to know that, nor does anyone else.'

'I feel like a fraud…' Her fingers tightened around her glass. 'I hate the pretence…It all seems so sordid.'

'It's not ideal,' he agreed. 'But it's all we have.'

All we have is hatred and bitterness, she thought with a deep pang of regret—hatred and bitterness and the stain of her sin lying between them indelibly.

'Carlo and Milana will join us tomorrow,' he said into the stiff silence.

'Yes…Giulia told me.'

'Will you be OK with that?' he asked, watching her steadily.

She looked away. 'Of course.'

'I don't want my mother to be upset.'

What about me? What about how upset I feel right now?

'I understand,' she said through bloodless lips.

'You look tired,' he said. 'My mother will understand if you go to bed without saying goodnight.'

She got to her feet and made her way to the door.

'My mother has put us in adjoining rooms,' he said as her hand reached for the knob.

She turned to face him, her hand slipping off the door knob as she did so.

'Don't look so worried, Anna,' he taunted her with a

smile that didn't quite make the distance to his eyes. 'I will make sure the door is locked securely on my side so you can rest without fear of an intruder.'

'I told you I'm not afraid of you.'

He gave a snort of something that sounded like scornful laughter. 'Then maybe you should be,' he said, lifting his glass to his lips. 'I would be in your place.'

She turned on her heel, unwilling to face the derision in his expression, her heart fluttering in her chest at the glint of malice in his dark, hooded gaze.

Anna was the last to join the gathering of guests in the sitting room the next evening. Sammy had been fractious most of the day and took longer than usual to settle, which left her little time to prepare for the dinner.

She showered briefly and slipped into a baby-blue gown with silver diamanté shoe-string straps which highlighted the clear blue of her eyes and the platinum blonde of her hair. She dusted her cheeks with a fine powder and applied a minimum of lipstick and smoky grey eye-shadow before scooping her hair up off her neck in a casual but elegant knot.

She took a deep, calming breath and made her way downstairs, her stomach tightening with each step that brought her closer to where the Ventressi family was gathered waiting for her.

'Anna.' Giulia was the first to greet her as she came in. 'Come and meet my husband, Pietro. I don't think you met him the last time you were in Italy.'

Anna smiled shyly at the handsome man who held out his hand to her, his dark eyes shining with welcome. 'How do you do, Anna? My wife has told me much about you.'

Anna was very conscious of the silent figure of Lucio standing to one side as Jovanna came forward. 'Anna, you look magnificent this evening, doesn't she, Lucio?'

'Indeed.'

'Carlo.' Jovanna turned to her younger son, who was standing near the drinks trolley with his arm around his obviously pregnant wife. 'Where are your manners? Introduce Milana to Anna.'

Carlo came across the room and mumbled his way through the introduction without managing to maintain eye contact once.

Milana's English was not as fluent as everyone else's, which made conversing with her difficult, and she appeared to be rather shy, holding on to her husband's hand the whole time as if frightened to let him go.

Dinner was announced by a member of the Ventressi household staff and Anna found herself being escorted by Lucio, his hand on the small of her back to guide her through to the opulent dining room.

She took her seat beside Lucio but was shocked to find Carlo was seated exactly opposite. She rose in her chair but Lucio's hand came down on her shoulder and she sat back down and lowered her eyes to stare at the table.

Jovanna was in her element with her family gathered around her, happiness shining from her black button eyes. 'It is so wonderful to have Anna with us once more.' She reached out to squeeze Anna's hand. 'And my beautiful grandson, Sammy, who bears an uncanny resemblance to his father at that age. All that fuss over going to bed reminds me so much of Lucio. He was always so stubborn and determined.'

Anna gave a weak smile and out of the corner of her eye saw Carlo's stricken features as he examined the contents of his glass with fierce intent.

'Mind you, Giulia was always a little pig-headed,' Jovanna continued with a fond look towards her daughter.

'Thank you, Mama, but what about Carlo?' Giulia protested with a pout. 'He hasn't exactly been an angel all these years.'

Jovanna smiled. 'No, but the love of a good woman has transformed him, hasn't it, Carlo?'

Carlo's mouth stretched into an uncomfortable smile as he put his arm around his wife's shoulders. 'I am very lucky, yes.'

'Where would any of us be without our beautiful wives?' Pietro said, smiling at Giulia with such love in his eyes it made Anna's heart squeeze. How she wished Lucio loved her! It seemed so unfair for her to love him so deeply when he no longer felt anything for her.

The conversation switched to other topics, to Anna's relief. She listened without participating and when Carlo lapsed into Italian for Milana's benefit she took the opportunity to privately reflect on the family around the table.

Lucio was silent unless someone spoke directly to him, a fact which hadn't escaped his mother's notice. Anna could see the tiny frown between Jovanna's brows as she watched the interaction between her children and their partners.

She felt Jovanna's watchful gaze resting on her once or twice and did her best to meet it with a smile and a bland expression which she hoped gave no clue to what she was feeling inside.

Giulia was her happy, engaging self, basking in the love of her handsome husband, her glowing beauty a testimony to Pietro's devotion.

Anna turned her attention to Milana, coming to the immediate conclusion that she was quite clearly a young woman in love. She spent a great deal of time gazing up into Carlo's face, her big brown eyes almost liquid with love and admiration, a love and admiration that was very evidently returned if Carlo's expression was to be believed.

Anna disguised her inward sigh. No wonder Lucio had insisted she stay silent about Sammy being Carlo's son.

Such an announcement would only damage, if not destroy, the young couple's relationship, especially since Milana was just weeks away from giving birth. She remembered all too well the fragility of her emotions in the weeks leading up to Sammy's arrival. It would be unnecessarily cruel to inform Carlo's bride of his role four years ago in the break-up of his brother's relationship with her. It was in the past and would have to stay there where it belonged.

Once the meal was finished everyone moved back to the sitting room where cognacs and coffees were poured. Anna sat as far away from Lucio as she could, her *demitasse* of coffee untouched by her side on a small table.

Giulia came over and sat with an exhausted flop on the sofa beside her. 'God, I'm tired. The twins were hell on legs today and even Antonio was fretful for most of the afternoon. I don't know what I'd do without Pietro to help me.' She gave a rueful grimace. 'Sorry, Anna. That was unspeakably insensitive of me. It must have been so difficult without Lucio to help you with Sammy.'

Anna gave a wan smile. 'I got by.'

'How is Jenny?' Giulia changed the subject diplomatically. 'Lucio told me she has completed one year at university.'

'Yes, I'm very proud of her.'

There was a little silence.

'Carlo seems very happy.' Anna examined her hands.

'Milana is perfect for him,' Giulia agreed. 'He went through a difficult time a few years ago. He has always lived in the shadow of Lucio. I think he was jealous of him until he found Milana. He seemed to change overnight, but then love does that to you, does it not?'

Anna's smile was even weaker than before. 'It certainly changes everything.'

'You are happy now, Anna?' Giulia asked intently.

Anna found it hard to hold her look. 'Things have been…difficult.'

'It will improve.' Giulia took her hand and gave it an encouraging squeeze. 'You have been through so much, what with Sammy's health and then your miscarriage. Your emotions will be all over the place for weeks yet. Give yourself some time. Lucio will be patient.'

Patience wasn't something she readily associated with Lucio any more, she thought as Giulia rose to join her husband who was making a move to leave, along with Carlo and Milana.

Jovanna kissed everyone good night and made her way to her room once the others had left.

Anna stood by Lucio's side as he farewelled his brother and sister, secretly longing to escape to her room so she didn't have to face another heated confrontation with him. The front door closed as the cars drove away and she turned to leave.

'Where are you going?' he asked.

She drew in a tight little breath and turned back around to face him. 'I was hoping to go to bed, that is if you have no objection to me doing so?'

'No objection at all.'

She turned for the stairs once more and had only gone up four steps when his voice stalled her.

'My mother suspects something is wrong.'

Her hand on the railing tightened and she looked back over her shoulder at him. 'How do you know?'

'I know my mother,' he said.

She let the railing go and came back down to stand in front of him. 'Did she say something?'

'She didn't have to. I could see the suspicion in her eyes. She's nobody's fool, it wouldn't take much to figure out we have an empty relationship.'

It was impossible not to feel hurt by his description of

their relationship as empty, especially as her heart felt so full of love for him.

'What should we do?' she asked.

He frowned and loosened his tie as if it were suddenly too tight. 'I don't know. Try harder, I guess.'

'What do you mean?'

He gave her a level look. 'I will have to be more like Carlo and Pietro, I imagine. They appear to be able to convince those around them of their matrimonial bliss.'

'That's because they are happily married,' she pointed out.

'Yes, but we can act as if we are. That should take the heat out of my mother's suspicions, at least until we return to Australia. The truth will have to come out then, of course.'

'How do you propose to go about convincing them of what just isn't there any more?'

He compressed his lips together as if in deep thought. 'We are only here for two weeks. It shouldn't be too hard to conduct a civil relationship in the presence of others.'

'Your idea of civility is likely to be somewhat different from mine.'

'Perhaps, but then your idea of what constitutes acceptable behaviour in a marriage partner will also quite likely differ from mine.'

'Meaning?'

He gave her a contemptuous look. 'I saw the way you were making eyes at Carlo all evening.'

'*What?*' She gaped at him incredulously.

'He did his best to ignore you but I could see the strain on his face.'

Anna could barely speak for anger at his misinterpretation of the evening's events.

'Do you think he would leave Milana for you?' he asked.

'He is happily married and will not be so stupid this time to fall for your charms.'

'I have no intention of becoming involved with Carlo,' she bit out. 'Nor do I have any intention of continuing this pointless discussion with you.' She spun away but before she could take two steps he was beside her, his hand around her wrist bringing her up short.

'But I have not finished talking to you.' His eyes glittered with something dark and dangerous and her heart gave a tiny flutter behind the wall of her chest.

'I want to go to bed,' she said. 'Alone.'

'But we are married, *cara*,' he drawled. 'What will the servants say if we do not share the same room?'

'Your mother gave us two rooms,' she said. 'Everyone knows I had…I've been…unwell.'

'Ah, but you are not unwell now. Your doctor assured me you would be back to normal by now.'

'I don't want to sleep with you.'

'Are you sure about that?' His dark gaze flicked to the thrust of her peaking breasts, clearly visible through the light chiffon of her dress.

'You said yourself our relationship is empty,' she said. 'What would be the point in prolonging the agony?'

'I would rather you slept with me, a man you hate, than Carlo, a man who belongs to someone else.'

'I do not want to sleep with Carlo!'

'Then you shall sleep with me.' He scooped her up in his arms.

'Put me down!' she said.

'Keep your voice down, Anna,' he said. 'The servants will hear you.'

'I don't care who hears me!'

He took the stairs two at a time, his arms like steel around her.

'Lucio, I will scream if you don't put me down.'

He shouldered open his bedroom door and kicked it shut behind him, dropping her unceremoniously on the bed.

'I do not want my mother to witness one of our monumental arguments,' he said.

She scrambled off the bed.

He gave a deep rumble of laughter that sent shivers of reaction up along her quivering spine, his dark eyes glinting salaciously.

'You are so touchingly coy, but we both know what you want.'

In spite of her determination to hold him off a sudden spurt of desire leaked into her belly at his rakish look. She felt her legs sag beneath her at the fire in his eyes, her fingers curling into her palms as he stepped towards her.

'Don't...please.' Her voice came out on a croak.

He trapped her with his hands either side of her head as she leant back against the wall, his eyes holding hers like the force of a powerful magnet.

'Don't what, Anna?' he asked. 'Kiss you?' He pressed a soft kiss to the edge of her mouth, his touch so gentle it made her lips start to buzz in anticipation.

She drew in a catching breath as his mouth covered hers, his lips firmer this time, his tongue unfolding to dip between her lips to taste her. She could feel her resolve slipping out of her reach. Her need for him rose like a rushing tide, sending her pulse into a type of frenzy as he pressed her even further against the wall. She felt him against her, the hardened length of him bold and insistent, and her mouth flowered open beneath the increasing pressure of his.

He slipped the thin straps of her dress down, the soft glide of fabric across her sensitised skin heightening her need for his hands and mouth on her exposed flesh.

She sucked in a rasping breath as his tongue encircled her tightened nipple, taking it into his warm mouth and drawing on it. She felt the graze of his teeth and her stomach turned over with delight, his touch neither gentle nor rough but somewhere deliciously in between.

He turned her from the wall to lay her back on the bed, one of his hands wrenching at his shirt as he bent his knee on the mattress.

Her hands went to his belt as his went to the zip at the back of her dress, each of their movements hurried, frantic, hungry. Her dress was pushed roughly out of the way, his shoes thudded to the floor, echoing her own, and his hands slid to her thighs to hold her steady for his invasion.

Anna felt his last minute restraint and held him to her with desperate fingers, not wanting him to pull away when she needed him so much. 'Don't stop now!' she pleaded with him unashamedly, arching her body to find him once more.

He groaned as she connected with him, her silky warmth a temptation he could no longer resist. He surged into her with a guttural sound at the back of his throat, pleasure fizzing through him as her inner walls enclosed him tightly.

He heard the hectic sound of her breathing, felt the tensing of her slim body as she came closer and closer to the point of release, her soft whimpering cries thrilling him immeasurably. He felt her tip over the edge and held her to him as she quivered, the contraction of her intimate muscles sending him on his own journey to paradise with deep shuddering groans of completion.

He held her within the circle of his arms, unwilling to release her until he could safely school his features back into cool indifference. He couldn't allow her to see how much he needed her. She had almost destroyed him in the past—he had no intention of letting her have a second attempt. It sickened him to think of a future without her, but even more sickening would be watching her hatred for him grow to unmanageable proportions.

He knew she still felt something for Carlo; he'd seen it

in her eyes as they continually sought his brother. She had probably been checking for his likeness to Sammy. How ironic that it was he, Lucio, who carried the most likeness!

It had been painful to watch Carlo squirming uncomfortably in his seat, his guilt over the past almost palpable. Lucio wondered if Anna would break her word and inform Carlo that the son he thought was his older brother's was actually his.

Could he trust her to keep quiet?

Anna opened her eyes to find Lucio's dark, brooding gaze on her, his expression characteristically indecipherable.

'What are you thinking?' she asked.

Something flickered briefly in his eyes before he lowered them to the soft bow of her mouth. 'It is never wise to ask a man that, *cara*,' he chided her gently. 'For you might be disappointed in his answer.'

'Try me.'

His eyes returned to hers, the line of his mouth taut. 'Believe me, Anna, you would not want to know what is going on in my head right now. What you should be more concerned with is what is going on in my body.'

She opened her mouth to ask him what he meant but before she could frame the words he pressed her back down on the mattress and his hardened body told her in no uncertain terms exactly what he was referring to.

CHAPTER TWELVE

DURING the afternoon of the next day Jovanna offered to take Sammy to the zoo so Anna and Lucio could spend some time together.

Anna was in no doubt of Jovanna's motivations; she had personally witnessed the speculative looks cast her way for most of the morning. However, once his mother had left with Sammy, Lucio informed her he had some work to attend to which could no longer be ignored.

She fought back her disappointment, unwilling to show him how much his rejection hurt. She had hoped after last night that he would let down his guard and allow himself to feel something deeper for her, but her hopes were continually crushed by the cool demeanour of his face whenever she caught him looking at her.

She sighed as the door closed on his exit, the huge house seeming empty without his intimidating presence. She wandered from room to room, smiling politely at the household staff, who hovered about offering her drinks and food in their faltering English.

She eventually retreated to her room, lying on her bed with the hope of sleeping away the boredom of the afternoon. She leafed through a book but her eyes refused to close and she lay there, fighting back tears of regret at how complicated her life had become.

She heard someone knocking at the door, and thinking it was one of the staff intent on feeding her yet again, got to her feet and opened it with a conciliatory smile.

Her smile instantly faded when Carlo stepped into her

room and shut the door behind him. 'What are you doing here?' she asked through a strangled throat.

He leant back against the door as if to block her exit. 'I need to talk to you.'

Her hands fluttered to her neck in a nervous gesture. 'I don't think this is such a good idea. What if Lucio were to find you here?'

'What I have to say won't take long. I have agonised over this for four years so please hear me out.'

Anna swallowed her unease as she witnessed the tortured expression on his face. His normally tanned features were pale, his mouth turned down at the corners, his eyes shadowed with remorse. He dragged a hand through his hair in a gesture so like his brother she found it almost painful to watch.

'I have something to tell you which I should have told you a long time ago,' he said.

Anna stood silently watching him, her expression guarded.

He moved away from the door to pace the floor, the sound of his feet on the carpet echoing in her head with sickening dull throbs.

'I don't know how to tell you this, Anna.' He turned his distressed expression towards her.

'Tell me…what?' Her throat tightened as she took an unsteady breath.

His dark eyes filled with pain. 'I didn't sleep with you that night.'

His words fell into the silence like a nuclear explosion, the aftershocks of his statement rocketing through her, making her head swim and her thoughts collide against one another painfully.

She opened and closed her mouth but no sound came out.

Carlo took a shuddering breath and continued. 'I laced your drink with a drug. I was insanely jealous of Lucio's engagement to you. I had gone from one disastrous relationship to another and when he met you and presented you to the family as his future bride I decided to put a stop to it.'

'Oh, dear God.' She finally found her voice and sank to the bed behind her. 'Oh, my dear God.'

He gave her a pained look. 'You drank the champagne and once it sedated you I...I removed your clothes and took the pictures.'

She made a choked sound in her throat.

'I'm ashamed to say I did not feel any real guilt over what I did until I met my wife, Milana. For the very first time I realised what my brother must have gone through in losing you.' His hand went back to his hair again. 'Then when I heard you'd had a child...'

Anna's mouth fell open as the truth finally dawned. 'Sammy is...' She gulped. 'Sammy is Lucio's...'

'He is certainly not mine for I did not have sex with you, Anna. You must believe me. I was bad, but not that bad.'

She was completely lost for words. For years she had tortured herself over her behaviour, even though she had no recollection of it, her guilt over the affair ruining her life and, even worse, Lucio's as well.

'Lucio must be told.' She got to her feet in agitation. 'He *must* be told.'

'No.' Carlo's one word stopped her in her tracks.

'*No?*' She stared at him in consternation.

'Please...' His tone was pleading. 'Lucio doesn't need to know. What I did was unforgivable but if it were to come out now who knows what damage it would cause?'

'It already has caused untold damage!' she protested. 'Do you have any idea of what I have been through? I thought Sammy was your son! For years I have flayed myself for something I didn't even do! How could you do it, Carlo? You didn't just wreck my life but Lucio's as well.'

He swallowed convulsively and his colour faded even more. 'Lucio believes Sammy to be his child, so what is the problem?'

She sank back to the bed and put her head in her hands, unable to speak for emotion.

'He married you, Anna. You have your chance at happiness back. Please don't take away mine by revealing what I did, I beg you.'

She lifted her tortured gaze to his. 'You have no idea of what you're asking, Carlo. No idea at all.'

'I think I do,' he said. 'I love Milana with everything that is in me. I know Lucio feels the same way about you. It is somewhat of a legend in our family—the Ventressi males love for a lifetime.'

'He doesn't love me.' Her voice came out on a whisper of sound.

'He loves you, Anna. Why else would he have come for you? He has never stopped loving you.'

'He thinks Sammy is yours,' she said brokenly. 'We used…protection so he assumed, as I did, that Sammy was conceived that night.'

'What sort of protection?' he asked.

She told him and he grimaced. 'I have had three near misses with condoms myself. The failure rate is often underestimated—especially if you're not careful. Sammy is very definitely Lucio's son; you have only to look at him to see that.'

She felt her stomach cave in. Sammy was Lucio's son! But how could she tell him if Carlo insisted she keep quiet?

'I don't know what to do…' She twisted her hands in her lap. 'It doesn't seem right not to tell him. He thinks such terrible things of me…'

'Anna, please. Milana is a few short weeks away from giving birth to my child. I beg of you not to reveal my wicked past. It would destroy her.'

'But what about me?' Tears sprouted in her eyes. 'Am I to live with this shame for ever?'

'You did nothing wrong.'

'Lucio believes I did.'

'Anna...I was so wrong to do what I did. I know it's impossible for you to forgive me but maybe in time you will come to see it as a youthful prank that went horribly wrong.'

'It went horribly wrong for me, not you.'

'Do you think I don't know that? I know it and it grieves me but we cannot change the past. Lucio has taken you back and you can build your life again.'

'He plans to end our marriage as soon as we return to Australia.'

Carlo stiffened in shock. 'He won't go through with it. He loves you too much.'

'How can you be so blind?' she cried. 'Haven't you seen the way he looks at me? He despises the space I take up; anyone can see it.'

'Please, Anna, let me have these few weeks,' he pleaded. 'Once Milana has our baby, things might be different.'

'Oh, Carlo, how can you ask this of me?' She brushed away the falling tears. 'After what you've done, how can you simply walk away from this as if nothing happened four years ago?'

'But that's the point—nothing happened four years ago.'

'Now you tell me, when it's four years too late!'

'I know what I have done and I am deeply sorry for it,' he said. 'But if you tell Lucio the truth it will tear our family apart. My mother would never cope with the shame of what I did; it would break her heart.'

'You should have thought of that when you laced my drink,' she bit out. 'What did you use, by the way? I had no memory of that night so it must have been pretty pow-

erful. You were taking an incredible risk—I could have had
an allergic reaction and died—people do, you know.'

'It was a recreational drug that causes short term memory
loss. I only gave you a small dose.'

'Thank you for being so considerate.' Sarcasm filled her
tone. 'But, in case you haven't already realised it, I was
already pregnant when you gave me that drink. I didn't
know I was, of course, but that's not the point. You weren't
just putting me at risk but my child as well.'

Carlo's face was grey with remorse. 'I am so sorry,
Anna.'

'Sorry is such a useless word,' she said heavily. 'It's so
easy to say but it doesn't change the past.'

'I don't know what else to do,' he said. 'I can't risk Lucio
finding out about this, not now. Too much is at stake.'

'You know you are very like your brother,' she said with
a touch of disdain. 'You have the tendency to only see your
side of things. You've told me all about your concerns over
the truth coming out but you don't seem to be able to grasp
the fact that I have a right for the cloud of shame to be lifted
off me. I have lived with it too long, torturing myself with
what I supposedly did, when all the time I was innocent.'

'I realise this is difficult for you—'

'Difficult?' She leapt to her feet and stalked towards him,
her voice rising in anger. 'Do you know what you are,
Carlo? You're a coward. Why don't you go right now and
tell Lucio the truth? Be a man, for God's sake! He needs to
know; he has a right to know.'

The bedroom door opened behind her and she swung
around, her eyes widening in shock at the towering figure
of Lucio standing there, his expression visibly taut with
rage.

'What is it I have the right to know, Anna?' he asked in
a voice of steel.

She stood staring at him, totally unable to speak, wondering how much he'd heard or indeed if he'd heard anything.

Lucio's dark gaze swivelled to his brother, who was skulking near the dressing table. 'Carlo?' The dark eyes glittered challengingly. 'Perhaps you would like to tell me why you are in my wife's bedroom?'

'I…I was just leaving.' Carlo took a stumbling step towards the door.

'Carlo!' Anna croaked in desperation. 'Don't go!'

Lucio's hard gaze lasered hers. 'How touching, *cara*. Your devotion to your lover is sweet after all this time, but have you forgotten he now has a wife?'

'Anna, I'm sorry,' Carlo choked from the door and before she could stop him he slipped out of the room and closed the door behind him.

The silence was heavy with accusation.

Anna ran her tongue over her dry lips and tried to sort through the scrambled disorder of her brain to frame the right words. As much as she wanted to tell Lucio the truth, she knew that unless it came from his brother he was unlikely to believe it anyway.

'Why was Carlo here?' he asked in a voice that insisted on a straight answer.

'He wanted to talk to me about…something.'

'What?' His one word had the force of a bullet.

'He wanted to apologise for…for taking the photographs.' She was pleased with her answer; it was close to the truth, perhaps not close enough, but a vision of the heavily pregnant Milana just wouldn't leave her mind.

'What else did you talk about?'

'Nothing.' She lowered her eyes from his.

'I heard you telling Carlo I had the right to know something,' he said after an uncomfortable pause. 'Would you care to enlighten me on exactly what it is I should know?'

She compressed her lips, buying time as her brain tried

to think of something plausible to offer him. 'He said…' she took a shaky breath '…Sammy is definitely your son.'

She heard his indrawn hiss of disbelief. 'How can he be my son?'

She bit her lip. 'He is absolutely certain Sammy couldn't possibly be his.'

'The only way he could be mine would be if…'

'Condoms have a considerable failure rate,' she said. 'I know for a fact Sammy is yours, even if you don't want to admit it.'

'Even if I were to have a paternity test it doesn't change the fact that you slept with my brother.'

'I was in your brother's bed, yes, but I did not sleep with him.'

'Let me clarify my statement,' he said with a malevolent sneer. 'You had sex with my brother.'

'Not to my knowledge I didn't.'

'Ah, yes, the repressed memory thing. Such a convenient way of absolving guilt by pretending it never happened.'

She tightened her hands into fists by her sides. 'Why don't you ask your brother for an account of that night? Why don't you insist on him telling you exactly what happened, starting from when he handed me that first glass of champagne.'

'I have already heard Carlo's account of that night.'

'Ask him again.'

'I don't need to. Your guilt is written all over your face and has been since I opened the door on your little assignation.'

'Carlo came to me!' she cried. 'I didn't ask to meet him. I don't want anything to do with him. He's a pathetic coward who thinks he can wipe away the past with a stupid apology that lets him off the hook while I continue to suffer the consequences of his…'

'His what?' He frowned.

'Nothing.' She turned away. 'I don't want to discuss this any further.'

'Anna.' He approached her and placed a hand on her arm to swing her to face him. 'I know you are keeping something from me. I can see it in your eyes. Tell me what is going on.'

She drew in a ragged breath and met his determined gaze. 'Nothing is going on, Lucio. That's the whole point. Nothing has ever been going on.'

She pulled out of his grasp and left the room, the sound of her hurried footsteps echoing down the upper hall and then further on as she clambered down the stairs. Lucio stood and listened until they faded, his brows drawn together in a frown, his heart feeling as if it had been clamped in his chest.

She'd said Sammy was his child but, if so, why wait until now to tell him? Like him she'd assumed Sammy was the result of her fling with Carlo, her guilt over his conception clearly obvious from the moment he'd run into her in the café.

But now she was insisting Sammy was his son. Even Carlo was convinced of it, as were his mother and the rest of his family. Why hadn't he seen it? And, more to the point, what else wasn't he seeing that he should have seen well before this?

He reached for the phone extension on the bedside table and punched in his brother's mobile number and waited for him to pick up, his breath burning in his restricted throat and his hands around the receiver so tight he was sure it was going to break in two.

But if what he suspected was true, the telephone's injuries would be nothing to what he was about to do to his brother's neck…

* * *

Lucio rose from his desk as Carlo entered his office two hours later.

'You are late,' he said.

'I know.' Carlo avoided his eyes as he sat down on the chair opposite the large desk.

'What's going on, Carlo?' he asked.

Carlo's shoulders slumped as he leant forward in his chair.

'I asked you a question.' Lucio's tone was unyielding.

Carlo lifted his troubled gaze to the piercing one of his older brother. 'I didn't sleep with Anna.'

The thick silence drummed in Lucio's ears.

'I…I spiked her drink…I wanted to…to stop you from marrying before me. All our lives I've had to wait second in line for everything. As the eldest you have been preferred in everything. Our father gave you the chairmanship and the responsibility of hiring and firing staff, but what did I get? A second-in-command position which meant nothing other than I must always answer to you. I was sick of it, Lucio. I wanted to do something that would change everything. I thought if I got rid of Anna I would then be the first to have a son to secure the Corporation.'

Lucio swallowed deeply and his fingers around the pen he was holding tightened.

'She was sound asleep when I…took the photos. I concocted the story about us sleeping together; it was a bit of fun. I didn't realise the implications of it until I heard she'd had a child—your child.'

Lucio swore under his breath.

Carlo flinched at the anger in his brother's expression. 'I wonder that you doubted it; Sammy is so like you.'

Lucio shut his eyes for a moment as the white spots of fury buzzed inside his brain.

'I'm sorry, Lucio…What I did was wrong…I cannot change that, but—'

Lucio got to his feet in one agitated movement, his hand raking through his hair, the line of his mouth grim. 'Do you have any idea of what you have done?' he ground out.

Carlo swallowed, his expression paling sickly. 'I have some idea.'

'You have no idea!' Lucio roared. 'You've wrecked her life! You've wrecked our happiness!'

'She still loves you,' Carlo insisted. 'I'm sure of it.'

Lucio sank to his chair in defeat, his head going to his hands. 'She can't possibly feel anything for me but hate. I have treated her so badly.'

'You married her, Lucio.'

'Yes.' He raised his eyes, the strain in his expression clearly visible. 'Against her will. She wanted nothing to do with me but I forced her.'

'She'll forgive you.'

'What fool's paradise are you occupying, Carlo?' he stormed. 'How can she forgive me? How, indeed, can she forgive either of us?'

'I've apologised.'

Lucio rolled his eyes in frustration. 'You think you can wipe away the past with a quick apology?'

'No, but I can't have the truth come out now. It would hurt Milana, not to mention Mama.'

'All you can think about is how it's going to affect you! You have not once considered how this has impacted on Anna. I loved her with all my being and you destroyed our relationship with your lies! How can I make it up to her now?'

'Do you still love her?'

'Of course I still love her! What sort of question is that? I have never stopped loving her.'

'Have you told her?'

Lucio tensed as he considered his brother's question. 'No...no, I haven't told her.'

'You owe it to her to tell her what your feelings are.'

'It's too late.' Lucio's voice was hoarse.

'How can it be too late?' Carlo asked. 'You have a son, Lucio. Anna is your wife—you have a bond that will last a lifetime.'

'I told her she would be free as soon as we return to Melbourne.'

'Tell her you've changed your mind. Tell her you want the marriage to continue.'

'She'll never agree to it.'

'Then if you're not prepared to fight for her you don't deserve to have her,' Carlo said. 'If you had loved her properly in the beginning you would have seen she was telling the truth. Instead you accepted what I said, never once listening to her side.'

'The photographs were—'

'You saw what you wanted to see, Lucio. If you look closely at those prints you will see how out of it she really was.'

'I should send your teeth through the back of your head for what you did to her,' Lucio said, clenching his fist by his side. 'For what you've done to us both.'

'It would be no more than I deserve,' Carlo said. 'But you'd be better served to fix things with Anna. She is the mother of your son and it's up to you to build your future. I knocked away what you had but it's up to you now to bring it back.'

'Get out of my sight, Carlo,' he said through clenched teeth.

'I'm sorry, Lucio,' Carlo said again. 'I wish I could turn back the clock. I didn't know Anna was pregnant or I would never have done what I did.'

Lucio's face was ashen as he faced his brother. 'I didn't know she was pregnant and, for that matter, she didn't either. I had made every effort to stop such a thing happening…That's why, when I found out about Sammy's existence, I leapt to the conclusion that he was yours.'

'Everyone has naturally assumed Sammy is yours,' Carlo said. 'There is no reason for any of this to come out. Think of what it would do to Mama to find out.'

Lucio gave him a hardened stare. 'I have suffered the shame of abandoning the mother of my child for four years, while you have gloried in your new-found role as the redeemed fallen angel of the Ventressi family.'

'I am not proud of what I did. I wish I could make it up to you.'

'You can, Carlo, by coming clean. Tell Mama and Milana what you did. Then, and only then, will I consider speaking to you again.' He opened the drawer on his desk and handed a document to him. 'As for your future in the Ventressi Corporation, that too is dependent on that revelation.'

Carlo's mouth dropped open. 'You're firing me?'

The line of Lucio's mouth was grim. 'Don't make me do it, Carlo, for you know I will. I hold the majority of shares since your last careless handling of the Naples development.'

'But Milana is…' Carlo's Adam's apple moved up and down agitatedly.

'Your wife is your responsibility, but Anna is mine, something I have come to realise four years too late.'

Carlo seemed to shrink even further in height as he stumbled awkwardly to the door.

'I will give you until this evening,' Lucio called after him. 'After that I will be taking matters into my own hands.'

Anna came into the sitting room later that evening once Sammy was asleep to find her mother-in-law waiting for her, a grim look on her face.

'Anna, I have some dreadful news.'

Anna felt her hand reach for the corner of the nearest

cabinet to steady herself. 'What is it? Is it Jenny? Has something happened back in Australia?'

Jovanna shook her head. 'No, it's Milana.'

'Milana?' Anna swallowed. 'Is something wrong with…'

'She's been taken to hospital, Carlo is with her. She is haemorrhaging badly.'

'Oh, God!' Anna's face was stricken.

Jovanna's eyes misted over. 'It's so awful. Carlo and she are so happy; I couldn't bear for something to happen to her or the baby.'

Anna reached for Jovanna's hand to comfort her. 'I'm so sorry.'

Jovanna gave her a watery smile. 'You are so kind, Anna. I am so glad you are back with Lucio again. He has missed you so.'

Anna wasn't sure how to respond so stayed silent.

'I have been so worried about both of my sons over the years,' Jovanna continued. 'Carlo was so…unpredictable at times.' She gave a little reminiscent and tearful smile. 'How that young man ever got to this age without a criminal record I have no idea, but look at him now. He is devoted to Milana and so looking forward to being a father…' She choked back a sob.

'I'm sure things will be fine,' Anna said, hoping it were true. She couldn't help feeling guilty. Perhaps Carlo had changed his mind and told his wife of what had happened four years ago. It was understandable Milana would be upset but surely not enough to bring on the baby this early?

'I realise Lucio and you still have things to sort out,' Jovanna said, breaking into Anna's thoughts. 'I have seen the way you both act around each other. If there is anything I can do?'

Anna gave her a wan smile. 'No, there's nothing anyone can do.'

'He loves you very much, Anna,' Jovanna said softly. 'He

was devastated when you left. I have never seen him so…destroyed. I think the only thing that got him through was his anger. Rather than admit to what he was feeling he chose the pathway of rage, not the most ideal way to deal with a break-up, but he refused to speak of it so we all soon learnt to keep well away from the subject. Carlo particularly found it hard; he used to be close to his brother but…well…' She gave a little shrug and continued. 'Men are such strange creatures, are they not?'

Anna gave her an ironic smile. 'Yes, they are very strange.'

The telephone rang at Jovanna's elbow and she snatched it up with a hopeful glance towards Anna. The rapid conversation was in Italian but Anna could tell by the sound of her mother-in-law's tone that the news was good. She hung up the telephone and leapt to her feet, her eyes bright with joy.

'Oh, Anna! All is well! Milana has had a baby girl by Caesarean section and they are both fine.'

'I'm so very glad.' Anna hugged the older woman warmly.

Jovanna broke the embrace with a flutter of excitement. 'I must go to them immediately. Carlo insists. Lucio will be back soon. Will you be all right on your own? I could call Giulia to come over if you'd—'

'No, please don't go to that trouble,' Anna insisted. 'I'll be fine on my own.'

Jovanna had been gone about half an hour when Anna heard the front door of the house open and the sound of Lucio's voice conversing in his mother tongue with one of the staff. A few moments later the door of the sitting room opened and one of the servants came in. She nodded respectfully towards Anna as she hastily removed the used tea things, her manner slightly flustered as she exited the room.

The door opened once more and Lucio stood in its frame, an inscrutable expression on his handsome face.

Anna felt her indrawn breath tighten her airway as he shut the door with a definitive click behind him, her nerves stretching to breaking-point as he strode towards her.

'Anna.'

'Y…yes?' Her hands twisted in her lap, her palms suddenly damp.

His dark brown gaze held hers for what seemed a lifetime and yet it could only have been a few seconds. Anna felt each every one of them thundering in her heart as she looked up at him uncertainly.

'I am wondering how to say what I need to say without you storming from the room or, worse still, storming from my life as you did four years ago,' he said in a voice she hardly recognised.

'I didn't storm out of your life,' she reminded him. 'You banished me from it.'

His mouth twisted into a grimace. 'You are right, of course. I sent you from my life with no thought to what other explanation there could be. I chose instead to trust my brother's account and, as a result, you have suffered unbearably. I am so deeply ashamed of Carlo I can hardly speak of it. I had no idea he harboured such ill feelings towards me, or that he would go so far as to…'

Anna stared at him. 'He *told* you?'

Lucio's expression darkened with anger. 'I had to practically force it out of him but, yes, he did finally tell me what happened four years ago, and I wanted to kill him for it.'

'He apologised,' she said softly.

He gave a rough snort. 'He did—and he expected everything to carry on as normal when nothing can ever be the same.'

She bit her lip, understanding the anger he must be feeling but so relieved he finally knew the truth.

'He has robbed me of my son's early years,' Lucio ground out. 'He has stolen my happiness with you and smashed it beyond repair. All these years I have fuelled my anger and rage towards you—the innocent victim.'

'Lucio, I—'

'I forced you into an affair and then marriage, both understandably abhorrent to you, and to cap it all I then got you pregnant and, because of my unforgivable treatment of you…' His voice broke and Anna's mouth fell open at the glistening moisture she could see in his dark eyes.

'I love you,' she said.

He brushed at his eyes with a rough hand and continued as if he hadn't heard her soft admission. 'As soon as we get back to Australia we will file for divorce. I will set up a trust fund for you and Sammy; you will not want for anything ever again. It's the least I can do. I have been thinking about how to deal with the issue of telling the rest of the family the truth—' he gave a heavy sigh '—and, as much as I hate to admit it, I think Carlo is probably right. Revealing the details of what happened will only cause further distress, most particularly to my mother and Milana.'

'I said I love you, Lucio.'

'As for me—' his shoulders visibly slumped '—I have to face my future without…' He frowned suddenly and looked down at her intently. 'What did you say?'

Anna smiled. 'I've said it twice already; do you really need to hear it again?'

He grasped her upper arms in a vice-like grip and brought her up closer. 'Did you say you love me?'

Her eyes sparkled with a challenge as she held his look. 'I'm not going to say another word until I hear what you feel about me.'

His warm brown eyes melted with emotion and his voice

when he spoke was scratchy. 'I have loved you from the first moment I saw you comforting Jenny outside that hotel four years ago. I thought my love for you had been destroyed but instead it grew stronger and stronger over the years. When I heard you'd had a child I wished with all my heart he might have been mine. When I first saw Sammy I felt such a knot in my gut for he looked so like me at that age it was almost painful to look at him. And when I looked at you I felt the most uncontrollable ache of desire and need. I decided I would have you on any terms.'

'You were rather ruthless about those terms,' she pointed out with a little smile.

'I had already decided to pay for Sammy's operation no matter what you decided,' he said. 'I just wanted to make it harder for you to say no to me.'

'I have always found it hard to say no to you.'

He smiled a heart-stopping smile. 'I am very glad to hear that as I am going to ask you to tell me one more time what you feel for me.'

'I love you.'

He crushed her to him, his arms like steel around her slim form.

'I do not deserve your love.' His voice cracked. 'I have done just about everything to destroy it over the last few weeks.'

She eased herself out of his bone-crushing embrace and gazed up at him with eyes bright with happiness. 'Then you'll have to try extra hard to make it up to me, won't you?'

'How do you suggest I do that?' he asked, bringing her back into the warm shield of his body.

She nestled even closer and gave him a wicked little smile. 'Do you really need me to spell it out for you?'

His body leapt against hers and he gave her an answering smile. 'You know something, *cara*? There are occasions when I think words are a complete waste of time. I speak several languages but right at this moment my brain does not want to search for the right words to use in any of them.'

'What will you do then if words fail you?' she asked with a glint of mischief.

He lowered his mouth to hers and spoke just above her waiting lips. 'I thought I might do this instead,' he said, and covered her mouth with his.

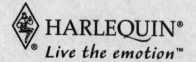

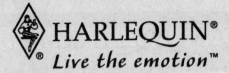

HARLEQUIN®
Live the emotion™

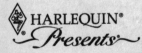

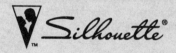